Joe felt himself being sucked backward into the darkness

He hurled his weight to the right until he felt the solid connection of the wall against his shoulder. Glass-covered pictures of women holding calla lilies rattled in their frames from the impact.

Just get out. Just don't remember. Don't ever remember.

And then the door swung open, and Emma stood before him, haloed by the golden light of a California Indian summer afternoon.

"What are you...?" she began, taking two steps toward him with those impossibly long legs of hers. "Are you okay?"

Before he could stop himself, Joe let his forehead drop down to rest on her thin shoulder. A minute. He just needed a minute and then he could talk to her and pretend everything was normal. He breathed in the warm, peaceful scent of the shampoo she used and, just for a moment, he was himself again.

Joe felt himself losing control, backward into the darkness.

He pulled himself into the light and to the pain explosion of the light exploded in his head. Please a sharp pain of wonind his head and it was impossible to see damo the impact.

Please get out Joe didn't know how there was silence.

And then the door swung open and forms sort of before him, backlit by the golden tinge of a hallway golden shimmer of morning.

When she got out of the wagon, hurled two steps toward him then froze almost to the very ground in his feet. Are you sure?

Before he could answer, Joe felt his head spinning and then closing his eyes, and just shouting a minute his eyes traced his body and down his spine. Now he started everything with normal life seemed to fall in the silence where to say. Suddenly, the entire night in that room he was hurled back...

TRACY MONTOYA

HOUSE
OF SECRETS

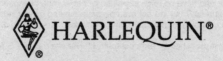

HARLEQUIN®

TORONTO • NEW YORK • LONDON
AMSTERDAM • PARIS • SYDNEY • HAMBURG
STOCKHOLM • ATHENS • TOKYO • MILAN • MADRID
PRAGUE • WARSAW • BUDAPEST • AUCKLAND

For Roselyn Rysavy
(the real Scrabble Champion of the World)
and Jerry Rysavy, the greatest grandparents ever.
Love you.

ISBN 0-373-88651-9

HOUSE OF SECRETS

Copyright © 2005 by Tracy Montoya

www.eHarlequin.com

Printed in U.S.A.

ABOUT THE AUTHOR

Harlequin Intrigue author Tracy Montoya is a magazine editor for a crunchy nonprofit in Washington, D.C., though at present she's telecommuting from her house in Seoul, Korea. She lives with a psychotic cat, a lovable yet daft Lhasa apso and a husband who's turned their home into the Island of Lost/Broken/Strange-Looking Antiques. A member of the National Association of Hispanic Journalists and the Society of Environmental Journalists, Tracy has written about everything from Booker Prize-winning poet Martín Espada to socially responsible mutual funds to soap opera summits. Her articles have appeared in a variety of publications, such as *Hope, Utne Reader, Satya, YES!, Natural Home,* and *New York Naturally.* Prior to launching her journalism career, she taught in an under-resourced school in Louisiana through the AmeriCorps Teach for America program.

Tracy holds a master's degree in English literature from Boston College and a B.A. in the same from St. Mary's University. When she's not writing, she likes to scuba dive, forget to go to kickboxing class, wallow in bed with a good book or get out her new guitar with a group of friends and pretend she's Suzanne Vega.

She loves to hear from readers—e-mail TracyMontoya@aol.com or visit www.tracymontoya.com.

Books by Tracy Montoya

HARLEQUIN INTRIGUE
750—MAXIMUM SECURITY
877—HOUSE OF SECRETS*

*Mission: Family

CAST OF CHARACTERS

Joe Lopez—After witnessing his mother's murder at age ten, his mind coped by erasing all memory of early childhood. But now, the man without a past is seeking answers—or maybe they're seeking him.

Emma Jensen Reese—An English professor at St. Xavier University, Emma learns that the old Victorian home she so lovingly restored was the house where Joe spent his childhood.

Daniela and Ramon Lopez—Twenty-five years ago, they were murdered, leaving behind four children who are still searching for answers...and each other.

The Whistling Man—With a penchant for whistling Sinatra, he shadows Joe with an obvious intent to inflict harm.

Detective Daniel Rodriguez—A member of Homicide Special, the Los Angeles Police Department's elite detective unit, Rodriguez manages to show up whenever trouble comes calling. Does he really want to help, or is the detective hiding something?

Senator Wade Allen—An extramarital affair made him the victim of blackmail. Did he order the Lopezes killed to save his political career?

Amelia Rosemont Allen—Married to Senator Allen, Amelia will do anything to support her husband.

Mavis Richards—The "other woman" in Senator Allen's past has put the past behind her. Or has she?

Prologue

Twenty-five years ago

When the glass of her basement window shattered late one Sunday night, Daniela Lopez's face barely registered surprise. Mainly because she didn't feel any.

Daniela sat in the dark on the unforgiving hardwood staircase inside her Victorian home, only her eyes moving as they scanned the front door. Then the foyer. Then the inky blackness of her front hallway.

Silence.

Her thumb clicked off the safety of her off-duty Smith & Wesson—the only gun she had left after taking an extended leave of absence from work. At least she could be grateful they hadn't sent a real professional after her. The spectacular crash the intruder had made upon entering her house gave her a small bit of comfort. Maybe she'd actually survive the night. Maybe buy herself enough time to put the last piece of the puzzle in place, to put the ones who'd murdered her husband behind bars forever. To keep the rest of her family safe.

God, she missed them. She wanted to smell the sweet baby softness of Sabrina's hair. She wanted to scoop up both her twin boys, Patricio and Daniel, and read that ridiculous *Mike Mulligan and His Steam Shovel* book to them for the hundredth time. And, despite the fact that ten-year-old José Javier thought he was a man already, she would have held him close and sang him to sleep had he only been there beside her.

But her children were safe at her friend Jasmine's house. And she was here. Alone in the dark.

Creak.

The unmistakable sound of pressure on the loose board at the foot of the basement stairs told her she didn't have long to wait.

She trained her gun on the doorway to the kitchen.

A few more days. Just give me a few more days. She was so close to finding out who'd ripped her family apart as if they were a chain of paper dolls. She could feel it.

She heard a soft footfall on the kitchen linoleum.

And stay away from my children, she prayed silently.

"Mama?"

She nearly dropped her gun when the tiny, boyish voice called out to her. "José?" Daniela sprang off the staircase and vaulted down the stairs to the hallway. Sure enough, there stood her oldest son, bundled in a Lakers jacket two sizes too large for him. His big, guilty eyes stared up at her under the too-long bangs of his shaggy black hair. Light from the streetlamps filtered through the slats of the window blinds, illuminating the hammer José clenched in his right fist. No doubt it was the same hammer that had smashed through glass moments before.

"*Nene,* what are you doing here?" she

asked gently, switching on the safety of her gun. She pulled up the back of the gray LAPD T-shirt she was wearing and stuffed the Smith & Wesson in the back of her jeans.

"I don't like you all alone here, Mama." He crossed his arms, hammer and all, and braced his feet wide apart, his dark brown eyes all defiance. Her little man. "Not after what happened to Papi."

Daniela's heart clenched at the mention of her children's father. "*Corazon,* I need you to go back to Jasmine's. It's not safe for you here." She tugged him into the living room, where an inexpensive cordless phone lay on the end table near the terrible orange-flowered sofa the boys had picked out for her last birthday. "I'm going to call—"

"No, Mama. I'm staying here with you."

So like his father, in every good way. Bracing her hands on José's narrow shoulders, Daniela bent down to look her son in the eye. "Sweetheart, I need you to do something for me," she said. "I need you to go back to Jasmine's and watch over

Sabrina, Patricio and Daniel." His stout little form remained rigid. "I don't like being apart from you, either," she continued, "but I have to find out what happened to your daddy. And I'll only be able to do it if I know you're protecting your brothers and your sister."

He glared fiercely at her, then his lower lip trembled as he threw his small arms around her waist. "I miss you, Mama."

She wrapped one arm around him while pulling the gun out of her waistband with the other to keep it away from his clutching fingers. She set the weapon on the table near the phone and bent to hold her son.

And then she heard the faintest noise from the curving staircase in the front foyer. The kind of noise that sounded like something coming from the outside or something you'd imagined.

They hadn't sent an amateur after all.

She squeezed José by the shoulders, moving him away from her body. With her finger to her lips, she guided him around the awful sofa, over to the far wall, her fingers fumbling for the small level she knew was there. That was the thing about old Victorian houses—lots of drafty alcoves, dark places, secret corners where people could hide. And one of them lay just beneath her scrabbling fingertips.

Just big enough for one small boy.

José opened his mouth to say something to her, but she placed her fingers over his lips, then gestured for him to crawl inside the opening she'd uncovered. He shook his head.

Her cop-sense told her someone had moved into the hallway behind them.

"Please, sweetheart," she whispered. He must have heard the urgency in her voice, because he quashed his stubborn streak and moved.

"Don't say a word, my angel," she whispered as she helped José tuck himself inside. "Not until the police come."

Another footstep, this one closer.

"Turn your head, baby," Daniela whispered at the wall behind which her son lay. "Close your eyes." José could escape when the time came. Now all she needed was a miracle.

The softest exhale came from the doorway.

Daniela turned, stretching her arms out to make herself large enough to protect her boy. Time slowed to a crawl, measured in her own thundering heartbeats. Her head swiveled toward the doorway. A shadow moved into her line of vision. She threw her weight to the side. The man before her raised his arm and pointed at her pounding heart. Her body arced toward the end table. For a few exhilarating seconds, she was flying, her hand nearly closing on the gun that lay on the end table.

She wasn't fast enough.

Chapter One

Stumbling over a loose brick, the boy lurched down the well-worn path. The open doorway before him grew taller and wider and blacker, like something out of *Alice in Wonderland*. *But it was no white rabbit he was chasing.*

Urgency wrapped itself around his narrow chest, threatening to squeeze the air out of his thin frame. And even though he knew he had to go inside, he skidded to a stop, breathing hard. The doorway of the large Victorian house stretched and undulated above him.

He looked down at the scuffed white tops of his Nikes. He was small. Weak. And the house, which was so beautiful during *the daytime, frightened him to the core in the dark.*

"Mama," he breathed, looking down at his hands. They were the hands of a ten-year-old, and the sight of them made him feel that something was very wrong. They should have been bigger hands, stronger hands. Squinting his eyes shut, he willed them to grow into the hands that should have been his. When he looked at them again, he saw they had not.

He jerked his head up, and the scenery around him blurred and darkened. Then he was inside.

"Mama?" he called, pitching his voice as low as he could to keep from sounding like a crybaby, even though he felt like one. A floorboard creaked above him, and he saw a ripple of movement in the shadows on the stairway. A breeze blew across his cheek, sending the door crashing shut behind him.

He cringed at the sound and hurled his body toward the wall, seeking the security of something to grab onto. His hand closed around one of the carved wooden newel posts flanking the large staircase in the front foyer. He traced his fingers around the whorls and dips of the carved shape of a horse's head that had inspired many a boyhood fantasy of knights and castles and flashing swordfights. The familiarity should have been comforting. It wasn't.

His head throbbed with a sudden, sharp pain, and he pressed his hands against the sides of his skull. "Nooo," he moaned, not wanting to go any farther into the house, not wanting to see. Then his mother's face floated into his line of vision, a pale oval framed by dark hair pulled back into a loose ponytail. The slight lines around her large, brown eyes crinkled with love and concern as she looked at him. They also held an unspoken message—he shouldn't have come.

She reached for him, brushing his hair away from his forehead with the softest of touches. "Close your eyes, José Javier," she whispered. He did.

He felt her hand on his chest, and then, with a vicious, sudden force, he was pushed back, back, back into a long black tunnel, away from his mother, away from everything. He scrambled for purchase, trying to climb out and save her from what he knew was coming. But his body kept sinking, farther and farther away.

A disembodied voice next to him, inside the tunnel, inside his head, whispered soothingly in his ear: "Turn your head, baby. Close your eyes."

And then he heard his mother scream.

"Sɪʀ? Sɪʀ!"

He batted at the fingers that gripped his shoulder and groaned. *Let go of me.*

"Sir, please wake up."

Let go.

"Wha—?" Blinking rapidly, Joe Lopez shook off the last net-like strands of the dream holding him under the waterline of consciousness. He scrubbed a hand across his face, opening his mouth wide for a loud, gaping yawn. Once he'd rubbed the sleep out of his eyes, the dream evaporated from his memory, and he finally managed to register the presence of one very flustered flight attendant. Her well-manicured hand was still on his arm.

"Sir, I'll need you to put your seat back and tray table in its upright position, please. We're about to land." The woman straightened, tucking a stray lock of her sleek, blond hair behind her ear. The scowl on what would otherwise have been a pretty face told Joe she wasn't happy with him.

"Sure. Yeah," he muttered. He snapped the tray in place, hoping she'd hurry up and go away so the other passengers would quit staring at him. Thank God the flight to Los Angeles wasn't full, so he had the entire row on his side of the plane to himself. Otherwise, he probably would have drooled on the people next to him. Or smacked them around. He wasn't exactly the lightest and gentlest of sleepers, and he'd been down for the count as soon as the plane had leveled after takeoff.

Once the attendant had finally left, stopping two rows up to harass some other poor schmo who had endangered humanity by reclining his seat back half an inch, Joe turned his face toward the window. Tiny cars rode along seemingly endless ribbons of highway, matchstick-sized palm trees, and the sparkling blue waters of the Pacific lined with yellow sand beaches. Los Angeles. Man, he hated Los Angeles.

But this year, the National Association of Private Investigators was holding its annual conference in this godforsaken city, and he never missed a conference. He never missed anything related to his work—even when it meant he had to come to a hellhole like L.A. Most of the women he'd dated had told him he was "obsessed" with his work, and as a result, his relationships never lasted. They wanted more attention, more flowers, more *something*. And he was never able to give it to them. But there was always work, like a faithful dog.

He wasn't obsessed. He just liked his job. He was the job. Lots of people he knew were the job. Unraveling cases was challenging, and nothing beat the feeling of taking a seemingly unsolvable puzzle and putting the pieces into neat, irrevocable order.

Okay, so sometimes really great sex beat it, but it had been awhile since he'd had anything or anyone approaching great.

Lucy Harrington, his last girlfriend, had told him he was "emotionally distant" and "completely closed off" right before she threw a dinner plate at his head and broke his brand-new high-definition TV set. That had not been great. And that had also been the last time he'd seen Lucy Harrington. Last he'd heard, she was engaged to some stockbroker from Carmel. He hoped they registered for plastic plates instead of china.

The plane dipped noticeably as the pilot hit an air pocket, and Joe's stomach responded by doing a little tap dance that— if he hadn't known better—he might have attributed to nerves. But of course it wasn't. José Javier Lopez didn't get "nerves." It was just L.A. Maybe he was allergic to it. Because one little city was nothing to be scared of, unless you feared rank smog and a proliferation of brittle, unhappy people who'd gone to see their friendly neighborhood plastic surgeon so many times, they'd become wall-eyed.

Joe rested his forehead against the Plexiglas of the small, oval window next to his seat. So if he wasn't scared, then why did he feel like he'd rather lop off his own head than get off that plane?

"Maybe," Lucy Harrington said inside his head, "if you weren't so out of touch with your emotions, you'd be able to talk about how you're feeling, instead of repressing everything and watching baseball instead."

Yeah, what do you know, Luce?

And for the record, basketball was his sport of choice. Anyone who'd been as interested as she had in becoming Mrs. Lucy Harrington Lopez should have known that.

What he wouldn't give to be watching a game right now, with a cold six-pack and his dog Roadkill sitting next to him. But instead, he was minutes away from landing in Los Angeles. He turned away from the window in disgust. He'd hated the city for as long as he could remember, and for the life of him, he couldn't remember exactly why.

Story of his life. He couldn't remember a lot of things.

"Ladies and gentlemen, the Fasten Seat Belt sign has been turned on," a voice called over the airplane loudspeaker. "Please return to your seats. We are about to start our final descent into Los Angeles International Airport. Local time is 10:37 a.m."

Joe's hand gripped the armrest until his knuckles looked bloodless.

Man, he hated this city.

WITH A QUICK GLANCE over her shoulder, Emma Jensen Reese shifted her grocery bags, the heavy brown paper crumpling slightly under the pressure of her forearms. He was still behind her.

Emma hadn't actually seen him close up, but she'd registered the baseball cap, baggy mid-length coat and penchant for whistling Sinatra. Was he dangerous? She didn't know. At every intersection, she kept telling herself that he would turn this time, that it was all in her head, that he was just some random guy who lived in the area and also needed to go to the Trader Joe's at ten o'clock at night because he needed eggs and had a craving for those chocolate raspberry jelly things they sold. But the thoughts didn't keep her from worrying.

Maybe she was overdramatizing the situation, but he'd been walking behind her for five blocks now. In the dark. The thought made her instinctively quicken her pace down Third, the heels of her boots echoing on the pavement.

Her ears pricked up as the faint footsteps behind her sped up accordingly. Emma's pulse followed suit.

Maybe she was in danger.

Ridiculous. She was being utterly, completely ridiculous. After all, she'd been walking in a straight line ever since she'd left the health food store, and Third wasn't exactly one of the most deserted streets in Los Angeles. Three cars whipped by her in succession as if to illustrate the point. She would turn down that short alley a few feet away—the one that threaded between a couple of high-rises and ended within a block of her Hancock Park neighborhood—and everything would be all right. He'd keep right on going.

She turned.

A few seconds later, so did he.

The thin, shrill notes of someone whistling "All or Nothing at All" hung shrilly in the cool night air. They screeched down her spine like the chalk sometimes did on her blackboard when she wrote too fast.

"Stupid, stupid, stupid," Emma muttered to herself, the words keeping time with her ever-quickening steps. The decision to enter the alley hadn't been one of her best. In a nutshell, she'd just acted like some clueless bimbo in a B-grade horror flick, and the person behind her had her just where he wanted her. And now she was going to die. She was going to die trapped in a horrible cliché.

Glancing back at him, Emma hugged the bags closer to her body, noting that he was still about fifty feet behind her. If she started to run, so would he.

Emma kept walking. Not yet. She wasn't ready.

She should have driven, but *nooooo*. She'd caved to convenience and had bought a gas-electric hybrid car instead of a wholly electric model, and so she usually walked on most errands out of guilt. No matter how late at night.

A cool summer twilight breeze blew at

her back, and she tossed her head frantically when her hair flew into her eyes. For
crying out loud, some gang banging hip
hop artist had been shot mere blocks from
where she was right at this moment, and
he'd had an entire entourage protecting
him. She had a rape whistle and a pound
of organic butter.

Emma glanced down at the bags she
held. And some free-range eggs.

Her calves ached from walking too fast
in her high-heeled boots, but she pushed
herself further and faster. She would not
die in that alley. She would not.

The faint notes of "My Way" floated on
the air to sift through her hair and disappear on the evening breeze. Mother in
heaven, he was closer now. Emma swept
her gaze frantically across her surroundings, weighing her options. She could keep
pretending she had no idea he was behind
her and hope someone would stumble upon her and come to her aid. She could walk
as quickly as possible through the rest of
the alley and go directly to one of the big
mansions on the next street. Or, she could

drop the bags and run screaming back to the nearest well-lit commercial area, hoping she could beat her pursuer. The latter seemed like the best option—if she went up to a house and the inhabitants didn't open the door, she was finished.

Choose.

The heel of her leather boot caught in a sidewalk crack, and her ankle buckled, causing her to lurch onto the carefully tended grass beside her.

She heard him laugh behind her, a low, rumbling, ominous sound.

An eternity later, she finally made it out of the alley, and she jogged to the nearest streetlight, basking in the glow of its warm yellow circle of light. People could see her. She was safe now.

And then she felt the breath of a stranger on the back of her neck, as someone behind her whistled "Strangers in the Night."

That was it. The next level.

Emma dropped her bags, her groceries spilling and rolling onto the sidewalk at her feet. Screaming "Fire!" as she'd been taught in the free self-defense class on campus last semester, she threw her weight forward, running toward the front walkway of her house, just ahead. Something rippled in the darkness, in front of the fat little palm tree planted near the street, and she didn't know whether it was a person, an animal or just her imagination. She prayed it was something that would save her. "Please," she breathed.

The silk scarf she'd wrapped loosely around her neck slid smoothly across her skin and fell away—whether of its own accord or because someone had pulled it, she couldn't say. Quelling the urge to look behind her, she kept running in her torturous heeled boots, scrabbling through her purse for that damned whistle on her key chain. She reached deep inside her for one last burst of energy, just enough to live through this…

Then she tripped.

Time slowed to a crawl as the ankle that had buckled earlier gave out once more. It was almost as if she were floating above her body, watching herself stumble, scream, fall. Watching her pursuer pull a Taser from the waistband of his grimy jeans. Watching herself scuttle backwards on her heels and elbows like a pathetically small and scared crab.

The moonlight glinted off the Taser above her. Attack. Immobilize. Isolate. The words of the self-defense instructor came back to her with stark clarity. The pavement cut into the palms of her hands. The sounds of cars whirring along the nearby streets and highways mingled with dance music and barking dogs. The breeze blew her hair into her eyes. And Emma waited, not moving, not blinking, for the man charging toward her to do all of the above.

His attack never came. He charged right past her, toward the squat trunk of the short, leafy palm tree in front of her home, several feet away. The darkness rippled again, and a second man erupted out of the tree's shadow, chopping his hands so both thumbs hit either side of her would-be attacker's wrist. The Taser flew into the air, landing harmlessly a few feet away from her. Emma scuttled sideways crab-style on her hands and heels until she could reach out and grasp it by its thick plastic handle.

She wasn't sure how to use it, but at least it was in her hand and not anyone else's.

The two shadows circled each other slowly, one with his hands clenched into fists, and the other assuming a vague, martial arts-looking stance. The one with the fists—the Sinatra freak—swung wildly, and the other man curved his body into a bow, effectively dodging the blow. He followed defense with attack, delivering a well-controlled blow to the attacker's temple with the back of his fist. A lightning-fast punch to the stomach, knee to the head and swirling roundhouse kick to the chest, and it was all over. Her former pursuer slumped to the ground, unconscious.

Emma zapped him with the Taser anyway. Or tried to. She thought she'd missed, but then the man's body jerked upward and he went still. Whether he'd been intentionally following her or not, she had a great story for the next Take Back the Night rally on campus.

"Are you all right?" the other man asked her, his face obscured by the shadows. He held out a hand to her, and she grasped it, allowing him to pull her off the pavement to a standing position.

"I'm fine," she gasped. "Thank you." She glanced briefly at her pursuer, who lay spread-eagle on his back, groaning like a child.

"Get inside."

Emma squinted into the darkness, wanting very much to get a look at the man who might have saved her. "Who are you?" she asked.

But all around her was darkness, and her rescuer was gone. A handful of dry leaves blew around her ankles in a crackling dance, and when she looked at the ground where her pursuer had fallen, she saw that he'd disappeared, too.

In the distance, she heard the sound of someone whistling, "Strangers in the Night."

Chapter Two

"Both of them? Gone? Even after you'd zapped that guy?"

"Pretty much." Emma pulled her reading glasses off her face and tossed them carelessly on one of the neatly stacked term paper monoliths on her desk.

"Creepy," replied Celia Viramontes, St. Xavier University's now off-duty head librarian. "But let's go back to your mystery man. You never got a good look at his face?"

Emma shook her head. "He just swooped in, saved my life—sort of, I think, depending on the actual motives of the whistling man, which are, at the moment, a mystery—and then, poof." She flicked her hands in the air to demonstrate said "poof." "He'd disappeared."

"Wow." Celia swung her legs up and thunked her Betsey Johnson sandals on a rare clean corner of Emma's tidy but always covered desk, tugging open one of the buttons on the wine-red jacket of her fall suit. "That's amazing."

Emma leaned back in her chair until the hinges squeaked and gave her best friend a look that had sent many a student cowering back to their dorm rooms. "I hate it when the freshmen start researching the Romantics. You get sappy."

Impervious to "the look," Celia ignored her. "And what were you doing walking alone at night with serial killers on the loose?"

That made Emma sit up. "Serial killers?"

Celia rolled her eyes. "*Hijole,* don't even tell me you haven't heard about what's been going on in this country? There are approximately thirty-five to fifty serial killers at work across the nation at any given moment. Do you ever watch the news? Pop your addled professorial brain out of the 18th century every so often?"

"TV rots your brain." She paused. "Except for reality shows, which are often very deep commentaries on human relationships in the 21st century."

Celia snorted. "Riiiiight. Pick up a newspaper, then?"

Emma shifted uncomfortably in her seat. "Umm…"

"You know, living in the now for at least a few minutes a day can be good for your health. You can't just completely close yourself off like this." Celia reached forward and plucked Emma's glasses off the stack of papers from which they were threatening to slide off. She produced a case from a nearby drawer and neatly stuffed the spectacles inside. "You see where that gets you," she wagged the case at Emma. "Nearly assaulted in a dark alley by a psycho, that's where. You're going to be thirty-five tomorrow. You should know better."

"I'm not closed—"

"You are so," Celia interrupted, then threw her hands up in disgust. "It's a good thing you weren't shuffling around with your nose in a book down that alley as usual, or you'd have been toast."

"I do not shuffle," Emma objected.

Placing the glasses carefully on top of a short mahogany bookshelf, Celia rose from her chair and smacked her palms against the shiny wooden surface of Emma's desk. "You, my dear, are Rut Girl to that guy's Mystery Man," she announced.

"Rut Girl!"

"You teach your classes and spend the rest of your time grading papers and watching out for your mom, all sprinkled in with the occasional need to risk your life running errands in the wee hours of the night. I mean, I know you're sometimes restoring that old house of yours, which is cool, because you've got that Home & Garden thing going on and it's good to have hobbies, but get a life!" Straightening up, Celia tugged on one of the tight black curls that swirled and bobbed about her head and surveyed the room. "I know things with your mom have been tough, but you need time for you, too. You know, it's like Thoreau said: Live deliberately. Go into the woods. Suck marrow, et cetera, et cetera."

Emma couldn't help it. Celia had been the head librarian ever since Emma had earned her post teaching Restoration to 18th-century literature at St. Xavier's. They'd been friends since the moment they'd met, despite marked personality differences, so Emma should have been used to her dramatic tirades by now. But the fact was, this one hurt her feelings a little. Maybe because the assessment was so dead-on and something she pondered every year when her birthday rolled around. "Mom needs me," she said lamely.

"I know, hon, but even she's said she wishes you'd get out more," Celia said gently. She sat back down in the chair. "It's been a year, Em. Maybe it's time to let go a little."

Emma chewed her bottom lip, trying to ignore the tightening in her stomach. It still hurt so much to think about what might have been, what still could be. "It's been eleven months, Celia," she said quietly, staring at the dark screen of her desktop computer monitor. "And you know as well as I do that we're not in the clear until this year is up."

She heard Celia swing her legs off the desk and then felt a pair of hands pulling hers out of her lap. "I know. I don't mean to push, but your mom and I have been talking, and we're worried. You can't give everything to your job and then give it all over again to Jane."

Emma's eyes flicked to the photo of her and her mother on her bookshelves. Only someone who knew Jane Jensen Reese well could tell that she looked paler than usual, that there were new lines around her mouth and eyes, that her smart new hair-style was a touch too shiny and perfect, in the photo and every day in real life. "I'm scared," she whispered. She didn't have to tell Celia of what.

Celia clutched her hands tightly. "I know. I can see what waiting for this hor-rible year to finish up is doing to you. I wish I could help."

"You do, all the time." Emma stood ab-ruptly and grabbed her large bag, slinging the strap over her shoulder, which sank a little with the weight. "It'll be fine. That's what we have to believe, right?"

"Right." Celia flashed her a smaller, less bright version of her wide grin. "Well, come on. I'll buy you an early birthday dinner at Ca'Brea, and then you can drive me home in that snazzy new hybrid car of yours."

AFTER DROPPING OFF Celia at her condo, Emma pulled the snub-nosed Toyota Prius into the garage behind her house. Thirty-five. She was going to be thirty-five years old, and she'd pretty much spent all of those years—with her rigid routines and carefully planned schedules—digging her own personal rut, not just the past one. Rut Girl. Celia might as well have called her Deeply Entrenched Chasm Girl, with or without her mother's illness.

Thirty-five years old. As she tugged her overstuffed hemp satchel out of the car, the thought stopped Emma in her tracks. Tomorrow, she would officially be in her mid-thirties. Which meant that very soon, she'd be forty. Which meant it was high time she got out and broke the routines she'd been creating since she'd learned to walk and did something extraordinary.

But what?

To date, she'd achieved all of her goals. She'd earned her Ph.D. in literature ten years ago, gotten a teaching job and had risen through the ranks to become full professor of 18th-century literature at St. Xavier University, a small liberal arts college nestled in the palm-lined shadow of the University of Southern Caifornia in Los Angeles.

And now, her time was spent in a weekly routine that, as Celia had so bluntly pointed out, rarely varied, by day, hour or even minute. Could she possibly be any more boring?

Probably not. Even her name sounded like a stuffy old lady's—Emma Jensen Reese. Hah. "Hello," she mimicked herself aloud as she walked around her house toward the mailbox in front, "I'm Emma Jensen Reese, professor of stuffy literature at a stuffy university with a large rod stuffed firmly up my—"

Emma halted abruptly, the heels of her shoes sinking into the soft green grass.

The so-called Mystery Man was staring

at her front door. And in the daylight, he was what her students would call a hottie.

He stood before the baby palms lining the small patch of grass and flowers she called a front yard, his hands shoved into the pockets of a brown mid-length suede jacket. His face was lean, long, with sharp cheekbones and a straight, prominent nose that gave him a dignified profile. He reached up and swiped a lock of glossy black hair off his forehead, his hard mouth twisting into an expression of confusion. She knew confusion—she didn't have a reputation for creating St. X's most diabolical exams for nothing.

But it wasn't his questioning look that had caused her to pause in front of her home, dropping her chin to look over the tops of her sunglasses.

Emma, you and your stupid annual craving for adventure. This happened to her every time her Intro to Literature students reached the unit on the Romantics. Last year in October, she'd nearly thrown her entire hard-won career out the proverbial window to hike the Inca Trail and

build solar showers and other ecotourism
infrastructure with the Quechua in Peru.
And now, in her Keats-addled mind, she'd
turned a man who was probably canvassing for the Sierra Club into Indiana bloody
Jones. Shifting the satchel to better balance it on her hip, Emma stepped forward,
prepared to dispel this year's birthday fantasy, courtesy of the mysterious stranger,
once and for all. "Hello," she said to the
man. "May I help you?"

Emma's breath caught as he turned to
face her head-on. In profile, he was a hottie. But the full frontal assault of his face
was singularly striking. He didn't respond
to her question—just stared at her with a
pair of deep, startlingly light brown eyes
set under sharply angled black eyebrows.
Emma could only stare back.

A heartbeat later, it finally occurred to
her that the man could be dangerous, and
what she should do is fling her bag at him
and run.

But she couldn't stop looking at him.

"What do you want?" she finally managed, her mouth suddenly dry. Dark hair,

prominent cheekbones, tan skin. He looked Latino. Maybe he didn't speak English. She tried again, in Spanish this time. *"Necesita ayuda?"*

His eyebrows drew together, and he shook his head, stepping close enough to her that she should have stepped backward instinctively. But she didn't. "I don't know what I need," he finally said.

Oh, great. Like turning thirty-five-which-is-almost-forty, wasn't traumatic enough without having two close encounters with the mentally unstable in one twenty-four-hour period. Ignoring the fact that having a mysterious and rather Byronic stranger talking about his needs in the middle of your front yard ranked pretty high on the romantic meter, Emma shifted the satchel in her arms, readying herself for one good fling. She had no doubt that the number of research papers she carried with her would pack a wallop.

But she couldn't. Heaven help her, his lost expression moved her.

"Who are you?" she asked.

"Joe," he said.

Then he blinked and shook his head, scrubbing a hand across his face. As she watched, the dream-like cast to his golden-brown eyes faded. His jaw tightened, his brow furrowed, until the man with the tough, uncompromising expression before her bore almost no resemblance to the one she'd been talking to mere seconds before.

"I'm sorry," he said gruffly, turning his head away from her. "I don't remember— I don't know why I'm here." With a sudden, quick movement, he moved across the lawn to the sidewalk. "I'm sorry," she heard him mutter again. And then he was gone.

WHAT THE HELL was he doing here?

Joe stalked down the sidewalk, away from the giant Victorian house and the tall, pretty woman who lived there and now presumably thought he was completely deficient. "I don't know what I need." What the heck? His pickup lines were usually better than that.

The fact is, she'd scared him to death. Or, rather, that frilly Hansel and Gretel house of hers did, with the turret and brightly painted shutters and meticulously placed flowers and palms. Because both it and her entire goddamned neighborhood resonated somewhere deep inside him, in the darkest corners of his mind, where the secrets of his past had long lay dormant.

But she hadn't recognized him. That much was clear. There had been one moment when Joe had looked into her green eyes and thought she had, but then it had quickly become apparent that it was just her fight-or-flight-or-scream-holy-murder mechanism kicking in.

Not that he would have blamed her for doing any of the above, the way he'd been lurking in her yard. And the thing was, he didn't even know how he'd gotten there. One minute, he was getting into his rental car—a sweet Honda S2000 with a convertible top, a 6K VTEC engine that went from 0 to 60 in 5.2 seconds, and a roar like a topless rocket—and heading for the Convention Center; the next, he was standing in the yard of an old house doing his best impersonation of *Rain Man* and scaring some poor woman to death.

Maybe he needed a vacation.

Maybe he just needed to get away from that damned house.

As he approached the rental car, Joe fished his keys out of his pocket, then aimed the remote key chain in the Honda's general direction. A shrill beep signaled that the doors were now unlocked, and he was only too happy to crawl inside and slink away. As much as one could slink inside a fire-engine-red sports car.

That was twice now that he'd been out for a drive, minding his own business, only to find himself several minutes later standing in front of that woman's house.

That house. He'd dreamed about that house.

"Concentrate, Lopez," he muttered to himself, whipping a right onto Figueroa, which would take him straight to the Holiday Inn he was staying at near the Convention Center. The last thing he needed was to slip into another driving coma and boomerang back to the house like some sort of Mexican lemming.

The drive back to the convention was a

smooth one—light traffic, sunshine and warm breezes, and a killer ride, if he did say so himself. He parallel parked the Honda near the curb in record time, then cut off the engine and opened the car door. Maybe he'd have time to hit In-N-Out Burger before…

Holy Mexican lemming.

With one boot on the pavement and the rest of him still inside the Honda, Joe turned his head slowly, taking in his surroundings in what had to be the most surreal moment of his life.

He was back in front of that freakin' house.

Chapter Three

"Look." Emma yanked open the door of the flashy red sports car with such force, a few locks of her hair flipped forward into her face. With one no-nonsense flick of her neck, she sent them all flying back out of harm's way. "I don't know what you're doing here—again—but you have exactly one minute to explain yourself." As if barely escaping a violent attack and turning thirty-five-which-is-almost-forty, weren't enough, now she apparently had a stalker on her hands. Or her house had a stalker. Either way, it was bloody uncomfortable finding some unforthcoming stranger in her personal space every time she stepped outside, and she was determined to find out what on earth it was he wanted, even if she had to keep him from driving off by taking a screwdriver to that flashy car of his. Which probably got terrible gas mileage and had a poor emissions record.

The man she knew only as "Joe" scrubbed a hand across the side of his face, pushing his glossy black hair briefly off his temple. Wearing what appeared to be his trademark dazed and confused expression, he rooted his attention firmly on the house. Even when she stepped directly into his line of vision, he gave the impression that he hadn't noticed and was looking right through her. She wasn't sure what was more unforgivable— his lack of manners or his lack of fear in the face of her anger. She scared the St. X football team into doing their homework, for heaven's sake. Without Cliff's Notes.

But still he refused to even look at her. His mouth had dropped open slightly, and for a moment he reminded her vaguely of that young guy Diane Lane had had an affair with in that *Unfaithful* DVD Celia had made her rent a while back.

Narrowing her eyes, Emma rattled the house keys she held in one hand. Just because he looked like a hedonistic foreign guy with a thing for older women stuck in ruts didn't make him any less of a potential threat, but she was determined to get to the bottom of his behavior.

"Sir," she said, "I am speaking to you. What are you doing here?"

He unfolded his tall, lean frame from the front seat of the sports car. She stepped back instinctively. "I don't think I have an answer for you," he said slowly, his gaze remaining on her mango-and-burnt-orange Victorian home.

Emma's keys jangled as she looped the key ring around her forefinger. "Then perhaps you'd best concentrate until you come up with one." She raised her hand until a small canister attached to the key chain dangled before his whiskey-colored eyes. "This is pepper spray—the kind with UV dye in it, which will brand you as a marauding psychotic while the police track you down," she continued. "And if you don't answer my question soon, I will spray the whole canister on your head, and then I will beat you with its empty metal shell."

He blinked, then finally turned to look at her. For the second time that afternoon, his shuttered, cool facade snapped back into place, leaching the warmth and vulnerability out of his light eyes. "Look, lady," he said. "There is no marauding. Do you see any marauding going on?"

Emma's teeth clenched tightly with an audible click. She was just dying for an excuse to spray him.

"And furthermore—" He cut himself off, narrowing his eyes at the can of pepper spray she held. "You know, that's not a good brand."

She felt her anger slip a bit. "What?"

"That pepper spray. Sure, they say it doesn't wash off for three days, but in field tests, they found that a little peroxide will do the trick in about five minutes."

"But—"

"You want the good stuff, you really ought to order through the Spies-R-Us catalog." He closed the car door behind him and leaned back against it. "That stuff lasts for a week. At least. Can't even sandpaper it off."

Feeling out of sorts, Emma double-checked the safety lock on the pepper spray to keep from shooting herself in the eye and stuffed it in the cargo pocket of her beige silk pants. What kind of stalker gave you self-defense tips? Maybe she should have been more patient. Maybe she should stop behaving like a paranoid jerk and figure out whether the man needed help. After all, if he'd wanted to harm her, he certainly could have done so last night, after he'd gone all Bruce Lee on her would-be attacker.

"Well," she said with a sigh, "I apologize for threatening you with this inferior brand of pepper spray. Despite your penchant for skulking in my yard, you saved my life in that alley last night, for which I never got a chance to properly thank you. So. Thank you."

"I don't skulk," he muttered under his breath.

"What are you looking for, Joe?" she asked quietly. He looked up then, and something vulnerable and hurting flashed across his face. Maybe her asking was a reckless move, but he looked like he so desperately needed…something.

"You!" a deep voice boomed behind them.

Both of them turned their heads simultaneously toward the sound. A few feet away stood her neighbor, Louis Bernard, known to the neighborhood kids as Crazy Louie.

"Louis." Emma padded across the lush grass toward where Louis was half-hidden behind a spray of night-blooming jasmine. "Is everything okay?"

But he wouldn't even look at her. His entire being was focused on Joe. Jeez, no one paid any attention to her anymore.

Louis drew his silver caterpillar eyebrows together and rocked back and forth on bare, eggshell-white feet, which poked out from the hems of his brown knit pants. He'd missed a button on his shirt, so the right side of his collar stuck upward a little higher than the left, giving him a slightly hunchbacked look. His fingers were curled into the pages of the latest *L.A. Times*, which he crumpled against his chest.

"You go home!" he yelled at Joe with a childlike emphasis on each word.

"Louis, it's all right." Emma put a hand on one of Louis's bony arms, rubbing his thin bicep in a manner she hoped was soothing. "This is just Joe. He's my friend."

Louis swayed back and forth in time to music only he could hear, tufted locks of his silver and brown hair bobbing up and down with the movement. "Joe needs to go home," he said, a little more softly.

"He'll go home soon," Emma replied. Louis was the only son of her elderly neighbor, Jasmine Bernard, and although he was fifty-something, Jasmine had told her he had the emotional maturity of a child. He was also usually a gentle soul, not prone at all to screaming at her guests. Not that Joe was a guest or anything.

"I know Joe. I know Joe. I know Joe," Louis chanted.

Louis rocked and crumpled his newspaper, breathing as if he'd just sprinted to the ocean and back. At a loss, Emma continued rubbing his arm, until he finally started to calm beneath her touch. She glanced up briefly to find Joe staring intently at the two of them, as if trying to recall whether Louis really did know him. Obviously, Joe wasn't going home any time soon—he'd barely even blinked in response to Louis's rant.

Perhaps sending Louis away was her best option, to keep the poor man from getting too upset. "Louis, do you think your mother might want her newspaper?" she asked gently.

"I know Joe. I know Joe. Joe's newspaper," he chanted in response.

"Maybe you can go give it to her, and then come back after dinner and have some juice with me."

Louis grew quiet, though he continued to rock on his heels, then nodded.

"Come have some juice later, all right, Louis? After Joe goes home? You know I'm always happy to see you." Jasmine was always diligent about not letting Louis stay at her house for more than half an hour, but Emma would have gladly welcomed him for longer visits. Through some miracle and despite his disability, he played the piano with a virtuoso's touch, and she loved to hear him practice Mozart on the small antique upright in her sitting room. He'd been in a car accident as a child that had left him in his current mental state, but somehow the talent that was to be his had been left intact.

"Okay," Louis said, staring at something on the ground only he could see.

"Great, I'll see you later tonight." She gave him an encouraging pat toward his house.

Louis dropped his newspaper and clutched at the buttons on his shirt. "Come to Joe's house tonight," he muttered as he shuffled home. "Play in the tower with Joe and Daniel." And then he hopped up the steps to his house and disappeared inside with a slam of the screen door.

"Joe's house?" Emma scooped the newspaper Louis had left behind off the ground and folded it carefully until it was the size of a small notebook. She turned to face the man leaning against the car behind her. The "tower" Louis had referred to was most likely the turret on the east side of her house, which left her with only one question: "Who's Daniel?"

"No clue." He shrugged, though she saw something flicker in his eyes. Obviously Louis's words weren't as meaningless to him as he'd have her think. "You were really good with him, you know?" he said.

It was her turn to shrug. "He's sweet. I've never seen him yell like that. Does he know you from somewhere?"

He shook his head, his brow furrowing as the familiar confused look replaced the cocky one. "I don't know."

"Do you know anyone in this area?"

Pause. "I'm not sure."

"Did you grow up here?" she persisted.

His mouth flattened, and he flipped a palm into the air. "I don't remember."

"You don't—"

Joe abruptly spun on his heel and walked a couple of paces away from her, his broad shoulders heaving as he inhaled deeply. A moment later, he turned back, his hands shoved into the pockets of his black, flat-front trousers. "I know I might have alarmed you coming here, and I'm only telling you this because I can't promise I won't do it again," he began. "But something—" He took a deep breath, and then dove right in. "I don't remember the first ten years of my life. Not school, not my parents, not anything." He clenched his teeth and worked his jaw for a moment. "Something happened... It's gone. It's all gone."

He leaned against the side of his car, crossing his arms as he stared blankly at her house. "All I know is that the minute I landed in this godforsaken city, something kept calling to me, bringing me to this house. And I wish for the life of me I knew what it was so I could go back to blocking it out."

He pushed himself off the car in an explosive movement. "It's right here," he said, tapping his right temple with his fingers, "and I can't see it. I can't remember, but it's right on the edge of my brain. That man—" he gestured in the direction of Louis's house "—he knew me. I can feel it. But I have no idea who he is or whether I've seen him before."

Emma rolled the newspaper in her hands, feeling an almost irresistible urge to touch him, to comfort him somehow. But he was a stranger, and though her gut told her she wasn't in any danger, she didn't want to invite trouble. In the awkward silence that followed, she unfurled the newspaper, which was dated a couple days ago, and glanced at the front page. To her surprise, the bottom right photo was a clear shot of Joe's face scowling back at her, with a caption identifying him as one José Javier Lopez, a private detective who was receiving the National Association of Private Investigator's P.I. of the Year award for his work on several cases about which she didn't have time to read right now. Emma rolled the paper back up again, figuring now wasn't the time to bring up his fifteen minutes of fame in L.A. "Do you have any family?" she asked. "Someone who can help you put together the pieces?"

"There's no one," he said abruptly in a tone that told her he wasn't going to discuss *that* topic any further.

Darn it. First, she'd nearly gotten herself violently assaulted last night, and now she was standing here, in front of a total stranger who had been making unscheduled appearances in her front yard for the past two days, and instead of calling the police, all she wanted to do was help him. But before she could do or say anything more, Joe reached into the inside pocket of his jacket and pulled out a business card, which he held out for her to take.

"I'm sorry," he said gruffly. "I didn't mean to scare you any more than I already have. My name is Joe Lopez, and I'm a private investigator. I work mostly missing persons cases up in the Salinas Valley."

"Emma Jensen Reese," she responded automatically as she took the card from him. Like the newspaper caption, the card also identified him as José Javier Lopez, but he obviously preferred the more Anglicized "Joe." "Mr. Lopez—" she began, and then stopped.

He was standing at the top of the stairs directly in front of her door—her *unlocked* door—and he'd gotten there so quickly and quietly she hadn't even noticed. Before Emma could ask him what he was doing, Joe pushed the heavy wood and beveled glass door inward, stepping inside without so much as a "May I?"

She really was going to have to do something about these annual cravings for adventure before they got her killed.

THE DOOR SWUNG SHUT behind him with an audible click, bringing Joe back to reality. Somehow, he'd ended up inside Emma Jensen Reese's house, and Emma Jensen Reese was apparently still outside. And for all he knew, he'd teleported there, because he definitely couldn't remember letting himself in. One thing he did know—Emma Jensen Reese was probably calling the police at that very moment.

Knowing he should go back outside, Joe backed up until his body bumped gently against the door—but as much as he wanted to, he couldn't make himself leave. His eyes took in the muted burgundies and golds of the antique runners lining the hardwood hallway stretching out in front of him, the fluffy white furniture and the rich red walls, the rows of gold-framed photos and artwork. He noted with passing interest that his homeboy Diego Rivera's art was prominently displayed in more than one frame. It was a pretty house, an obviously much-loved house. It definitely wasn't a house that should make his hands feel clammy or his body want to lose its lunch.

But it did.

He focused on the rounded shapes and brilliant colors of Rivera's "Flower Carrier," knowing somehow that by doing so he was trying to avoid looking at the staircase.

Staircase. Now why would an innocuous little staircase frighten a big bad P.I. from San Francisco? Just to prove his masculinity—to himself if not to anyone else—Joe turned his head and scowled at the staircase. It was just your basic grand Victorian stairway—wide, wooden, flanked by two ornately carved newel posts.

And somehow, he knew that just behind it lay the doorway to a room he didn't want to see.

And then the world tilted on its axis. Really not wanting Emma Jensen Reese to find him doing a face-plant in the middle of her sitting room, he focused his entire being on the newel post nearest him. The air around it clouded, blurred, until all he could see was the smooth, round contours of the carved horse's head. He reached out with a swift, jerky motion and closed his now shaking fingers around the post. It felt familiar.

Turn your head, baby.

Snatching his hand away, Joe whirled around, searching blindly for the door.

Close your eyes.

Out. He had to get out. But his body wouldn't cooperate, and he felt himself being sucked backward into the darkness. He widened his eyes and hurled his weight to the right until he felt the solid connection of the wall against his shoulder. Glass-covered pictures of women holding bunches of calla lilies rattled in their frames from the impact.

Just get out. Just don't remember. Don't ever remember.

And then the front door swung open, and Emma stood before him, haloed by the golden light of a California Indian summer afternoon. "What are you—?" she began, her voice sharper than he'd remembered, but then she took two steps forward with those impossibly long legs of hers and caught him around the arms "Are you okay?"

Before he could stop himself, Joe let his forehead drop down to rest on her thin shoulder. A minute. He just needed a minute and then he could talk to her and pretend everything was perfectly normal. He breathed in the warm, peaceful scent of the shampoo she used, and, just for a moment, he was himself again. Don't ever remember.

"Joe? You know, the only reason I'm not calling the police is that picture of you in the paper. I figure the P.I. of the Year isn't highly likely to be a psychopath," she said, though her smoky, Marlene Dietrich voice had softened and her hands circled around his back in a soothing motion, much like she'd used with good old Louis earlier. "Let me take you into the living room, and you can sit—"

The mere mention of the living room was enough to make him lose it, and he pulled out of her arms to lurch toward the door. Just a few steps and he'd be outside, in his car, away from that house, this city, and the questioning eyes of Emma Jensen Reese.

Bursting through the sun-filled opening, he raced down the steps two at a time, feeling a trickle of clammy sweat slither down the side of his face to trail inside the collar of his shirt. He tried to get back to the Honda, but he only made it as far as the fat little palm tree near the edge of the walkway.

Joe fell against the tree, and he wrapped one arm around the thick trunk to steady himself, his stomach heaving as his body tried to purge the fragments of memory buried so deep inside, they burned.

EMMA FOLLOWED Joe through the doorway, pausing at the top of the stairs while he stumbled through her yard to get sick in the white sage she'd just planted around her baby palms a few weeks ago. He might be NAPI's Investigator of the Year, but he sure was odd.

She hovered over the top step, wondering whether she should go to him or not. He might be odd, but he was also obviously in pain, and not the physical kind. Maybe she could help.

And maybe it was none of her business. Number one, he had emotional baggage. Number two, he kept appearing on her doorstep and then running away again. Number three, he had emotional baggage. Number four, she couldn't help but think that he was good-looking, even while he got sick in her flower bed, and there was no way *that* would end well. Plus, she quite simply didn't have time for this, for him.

With that, she turned and went back inside, although sheer guilt allowed her exactly half a second to ignore Joe before it propelled her to the downstairs linen closet. Reaching inside, she took out a fluffy beige washcloth, went to the front bathroom to dampen it with cold water and headed back outdoors.

Joe was still there.

As she walked toward him, she noticed a black SUV with half-tinted windows sitting across the street and a few car lengths away from Joe's Honda. Someone was sitting inside it, and she couldn't shake the feeling that he was watching her.

Ignoring the prickle of uneasiness she

felt at the thought, Emma looked away. Better to deal first with the regurgitating evil you know than the potential spying evil you didn't.

Squaring her shoulders, Emma marched toward Joe's bent form, folding the cool washcloth and, when she reached him, placing it on the tanned skin at the back of his neck. She kept her hand over the cloth until his dry heaves stopped.

Swiping a hand across his mouth, Joe reached behind his head to touch the washcloth she was holding against his skin. She let her fingers slide away, and he pulled the cloth around his neck and let it rest in his hand. "Thank you," he said simply.

"Mmm." She took the now lukewarm cloth from him.

"I'm really sorry, Ms. Reese," he began.

"It's Emma," she interjected, not bothering to correct the "Ms." "And it's all right. Really."

In the awkward silence that followed, Joe reached into his jacket pocket and rattled his keys. "Well, I—"

"Look," she said, unable to shake the

feeling that he shouldn't go. Not yet. "Whether you remember or not, there's obviously something about you and this house. Is there anything I can do to—?"

"No!" Joe snapped, then winced. "I'm sorry. I mean, no, thank you. I just need to get back to San Francisco."

So he'd go away, out of her yard and out of her life. Just like that.

She licked her lips, her tongue sliding across the smooth layer of beeswax lip balm she'd applied earlier. "Well. Good luck to you, then." She tucked the newspaper under her arm and held out the hand not holding the clammy washcloth for him to shake.

He took it, her slender fingers almost disappearing inside his large, brown hand. "Same to you," he said.

Just for a moment, Emma let herself look, really look, at the man. She inhaled, breathing in the same air, standing in the same space, feeling the warmth of his fingers. He was a stranger. He was leaving. She'd never see him again, and, as had been the case with countless strangers whose lives had intersected hers for small moments in time, that should have been perfectly fine. But it wasn't. Something felt wrong. He wasn't supposed to leave. There was something unfinished here, and somehow she knew it was important that he tie up the giant loose end in his life.

She had to tell him.

Emma exhaled. Her fingers slipped out of his. "Okay, then. Take care."

He nodded. "You, too."

He gave her a small half smile, his light eyes crinkling slightly at the corners, and then turned away.

Just like that.

Okay. Back to the house we go.

As she was about to turn away from him, she noticed him jerk around suddenly to face her once more. Her eyes followed his line of sight, and she noticed a small hole in the wooden siding of her house. Had that been there before? She stepped forward and reached up to touch it, when another appeared right next to her hand, splintering the wood with its impact. What—?

"Get down!" she heard him shout behind her. And then something hit her in the small of her back with the force of a rock avalanche.

Chapter Four

The impact literally knocked Emma off her feet and sent her soaring into the air in a tangle of arms and legs.

She landed in the tumbled earth in front of her stoop. Her gardening shovel jabbed into the small of her back, and her head was surrounded by soft white flower petals. The force of the blow and the landing emptied her lungs of air, and all she could do was open and close her mouth like a beached fish, unable to take a breath. The newspaper and washcloth had gone flying with the impact; when she turned her head, she could see them a few feet in front of her.

Joe raised his head from where it lay between her shoulder blades, and it was then that Emma realized he was the unbalanced force that had hit her—and now he was lying on top of her. She craned her neck to look at him and opened and closed her mouth a couple of times, trying to convey with her expression her surprise, her gratitude that he'd pushed her out of harm's way and her fervent wish that he get the heck off of her. Simultaneously, she contracted her chest muscles a couple of times, but still she couldn't breathe.

"Gun!" Joe hissed, a hunk of glossy black hair falling into his amber eyes.

"Unnnhhh," Emma responded, greedily sucking in oxygen as her lungs finally, *finally* opened up. "Omigod," she gasped, pausing to take in a few deep, gasping gulps of air.

"Someone's shooting at us. We have to move." Joe rolled over so he was on the ground beside her instead of on top of her, using his body to shield hers.

Shooting? Her heartbeat went into triple time, while Joe looked as if he were discussing the weather, albeit very intensely. Emma wagged her head up and down in agreement and started shuffling as fast as she could for the side of the house, keeping low to the ground while still gulping air.

He gripped her elbow and began to crawl along the grass with her. Smashing flowers left and right, they quickly made their way to the side of the house, and then Joe pulled her upright and together they ran to the back.

"Oh, no!" Emma gripped the brass knob on the back door and rattled it, knowing what the result would be. "It's locked."

Glancing around, Joe reached into the inside breast pocket of his coat and pulled out what looked like two oversize metal toothpicks. "Duck here," he said, gesturing to the shrub beside him. She did as he asked, then noticed with some guilt that he was once again shielding her with his body. He inserted the picks into the keyhole.

"Isn't that going to take a while?" Feeling guilty about using him as a human shield, she stood.

He didn't even look at her but continued to work the lock. "You know, it's hard to concentrate when I'm worried about you getting your pretty head shot off."

"You say the sweetest things." When her sarcasm made him stop picking so he could stare at her, she crouched back behind the bush, if only to get him to open the darn door faster and preserve their lives. In an attempt to be helpful, she peered over the top of the shrub, keeping watch in case their sniper friend decided to come around the corner. Every slight movement, every noise rattled her, but she gritted her chattering teeth, clenched her shaking hands and swallowed the impulse to run away screaming like a banshee. Banshees probably made very good targets.

As Joe worked at the lock, Emma's breathing finally slowed, in tandem with her pulse. She couldn't help feeling somewhat amazed that she could feel even a smidgen of calm in a situation like this. Sure, adrenaline was still racing through her system like a hor-monal freight train, heightening her hearing and sharpening her vision of the world into bright, crisp clarity. But still, you'd think she'd be a panicking mess. You'd think…

She yelped when a sharp click sounded near Joe, like an empty gun being fired.

"It's okay," Joe said, still concentrating intently on her door. "That was just me."

So much for her Zen-like calm. Emma watched him work and willed him with all her mental energy to hurry.

Fortunately, Joe made short work of her lock, opening her door inside two of the longest minutes of her life. And here she thought the house had been burglar-proof. *Jeez.*

Gripping her elbow, he hustled her into the house, closed and locked the door behind them, and pulled her through the back enclosed porch and her walk-in pantry to the kitchen. She felt a burst of gratitude that the windows in that room were small and facing the neighbors, making them much more difficult for someone to shoot through. All the same, Joe sat down on the floor, his back resting against the under-the-sink cabinet, and gestured for her to do the same.

She sat and waited, toying with the sleeves of her beige summer sweater while he took a cell phone out of his pocket and dialed the local branch of the LAPD. When he'd finished, she hugged her silk-clad knees to her chest and asked the question that had been burning in her mind since the first hole had appeared in her newly painted siding. "For the love of God, I'm an English professor, and I'm nice. Most of the time. Why on earth is there a sniper in my front yard?" She struggled to keep her voice calm, but her confusion and, yes, even anger at the thought of someone wishing her ill—major, major ill—made her last word end on a humiliating squeak.

Joe snorted. "No clue, but if he were a sniper, we'd be dead. Not a bad shot, but he did miss."

It was a sobering thought, that their lives had hung in the balance between good aim and great aim. And Joe sounded so blasé about it. Emma stared at a knothole in the hardwood flooring of her kitchen and quietly freaked out for a few seconds, her arms still wrapped around her knees.

"You okay?" Joe finally asked after the silence had stretched out for too long.

"Can I get you something to drink?" Her brain had obviously gone on automatic pilot for a moment, because even she knew as soon as it came out of her mouth that the question was ridiculous, given their situation. The offer had been automatic, made partly out of reflexive politeness and mostly out of denial. People didn't shoot mild-mannered English profs stuck in ruts. Not even in Hollywood.

He shot her a look that was a blend of mild amusement, his mouth curving upward into a half smile that was starting to look familiar. "Sure. And do you have any of those little cakes?"

"Sorry." Resting her elbows on her knees, Emma pressed the heels of her hands to her eyes, as if she could block out the bizarre events of the last couple of days. "Apparently, my brain is still processing the fact that someone wants to kill me, and my mouth went on without it."

She felt him put a hand on her shoulder. His touch felt warm. "I know. I shouldn't be giving you a hard time. It's normal in a situation like this to want to pretend everything's fine."

"But it's not." With a sigh, she folded her arms across her knees and rested her cheek on them, facing Joe. "I've known you for exactly two days, and my life seems to turn into an episode of *Jungle Raider* whenever you're around," she said, referring to the only nonreality show she watched, an action-adventure program with a heroine who kicked booty on a weekly basis. "Why?"

He drew his knees up and let his wrists rest on them. "You know, you're awfully calm for someone who just got attacked twice in two days," he said.

Truthfully, even Emma couldn't believe the calm she was projecting, all things considered. "I'm having a hysterical hissy fit on the inside."

"Ah," he replied soberly, keeping his eyes on the back door. "Actually, I think you'll be fine once I leave you alone. I'm pretty sure it's me he wants, and you've just been in the wrong place at the wrong time." He flicked a glance at her. "I'm sorry about all of this."

"My own neighborhood is the wrong place?" she asked. "Look, James Bond, if today's shooter is the same person as yesterday's stalker, why was he following me home from Trader Joe's and taking such obvious pleasure in scaring me?" Her hand floated up to touch her collarbone, remembering the scarf she'd lost as the stranger had chased her. "At least, until he ran past me and tackled you."

"First of all," he said, ticking the points off on his fingers while still watching the front of the house, "he didn't tackle me— I wiped the sidewalk with him. Second, next to me is the wrong place. And third, yeah, I'm pretty sure he was after me. Scaring you was probably just his idea of passing time, freakin' perv. Remember that black SUV that was parked a couple doors down from you today? The one with the mud splattered on the license plates?"

Emma nodded, though she was sorry to say that she hadn't even looked at the plates. But then again, her eye for detail was at its best when she was reading a book, which was why she taught literature and he was the P.I.

"I've seen that SUV hanging around the entrance to the Convention Center, which is where I've been since last week," he continued. "Ever since that damn article came out in the *Times* with a picture of me. And I was walking around your neighborhood the night the three of us met. So."

Without warning, Joe rose from the floor in one smooth and sudden movement, pulling a large gun out of his shoulder holster, which had been concealed by his coat.

"What? What is it?" Emma whispered. Half a second later, the doorbell rang.

"STAY HERE." Joe tightened his grip on his 9mm Glock and headed for the front door. He had to give Emma credit—the gun obviously made her uncomfortable, but she hid it well.

Keeping low, Joe made his way through the front of the house, adrenaline preventing a repeat performance of his earlier theatrics as he passed the living room and central staircase.

Carefully peering from the side through the small glass windows on the front door, Joe was relieved to see two men from the LAPD standing there. They were wearing suits, which meant they weren't regular patrol cops, but they had both flashed their badges at Joe when he'd knocked on the window to let them know he was there. Slipping his gun into its holster, he opened the door and greeted the two with a pithy yet functional "Hey."

"I'm Detective Rodriguez, and this is Detective Landau," the taller of the two said. "We received a call from your home about possible gunshots."

As the fair-haired Landau silently reached up to adjust his yellow tie, something about their suits niggled at the corners of Joe's mind. Suits, suits, LAPD and suits. There was something he wasn't remembering, but then again, that wasn't highly unusual these days. Since his instincts told him the suit thing wasn't serious, he stepped aside to let the two detectives in.

"I called that in, but it's not my home."

He glanced at the street, taking in the empty stretch of blacktop where the black SUV had been parked. "I think the shooter is gone now." He closed the door behind them and introduced himself.

As soon as he said his name, Rodriguez, the larger of the two men, looked at him, really looked, and then started visibly. Joe narrowed his eyes at the man. Now why would the cop react as if he recognized Joe's name when Joe had only been to this armpit of a city once before, and that was only because a one-hour layover at the airport had turned into an overnight stay due to thunderstorms?

"What are you doing here?" Rodriguez asked almost in a whisper as he stepped into the entryway, not bothering to remove his sunglasses inside the house.

Odd question, considering he'd just been *shot at*. "NAPI convention," he replied, sizing Rodriguez up. The man was very close in weight and height to Joe's own build, but Joe figured he could take him if he had to. Not that taking down a cop was on his to-do list during this visit, or ever, but it was always good to know where you stood.

"P.I. of the Year," the cop responded. Obviously the man had done his homework. "Is that the only reason you're here, Mr. Lopez?"

Joe nodded, and the silence that followed stretched out uncomfortably. Rodriguez was seriously starting to creep Joe out. Landau, on the other hand, hadn't said two words since he'd walked in, but as he looked around the house and ran his fingers through his thinning blond hair, there was no question that he was the more benign of the two.

Just then, Joe heard Emma's soft footfall behind them, half a second before Rodriguez's and Landau's eyes flicked toward her. Rodriguez seemed to shake himself before taking a notebook and pen out of his pocket.

"I'm Emma," she said, stepping forward.

Emma's presence seemed to be a balm for the weirdness of the past few moments, and the rest of the encounter was more like one would expect a 911 response to be. The detectives interviewed Emma and him, recorded their answers in a notebook and walked around the house to check that all was secure. Landau removed three bullets from the house siding with an oversize pair of tweezers, bagging and tagging them.

Finally, the two cops were ready to leave, and Joe couldn't help but feel relief.

"We'll send some extra patrols past your house for the next few weeks, Ms. Jensen Reese," Rodriguez said. "It may have been a one-time thing, but since you had a suspicious person following you the other night, I don't want you to take any chances. Have someone accompany you when you go out for the next few days, and call me if you witness anything suspicious."

Emma thanked him, and then, finally, they were gone.

"Well. That was definitely bizarre," she said.

He nodded, watching through the windows once more as the men got into their unmarked Crown Vic and drove off. Something about their suits was still nagging at him, and not just because Landau's hadn't fit him right. Unless flood pants for men were coming back in.

"I wonder why Detective Rodriguez didn't take his sunglasses off?" Emma asked. "Nice suit, good manners, and then those big Unabomber glasses in a house that doesn't get all that much natural light. Doesn't make sense."

Unabomber, high-profile cases, suits... "Homicide Special," he said abruptly.

"Beg your pardon?" Emma responded.

Joe fought the urge to knock himself on the forehead. "I can't believe it took me this long to think of it."

Emma gestured to one of the fluffy white couches and moved to sit down. He sat on the couch opposite hers. "Okay, I'll bite," she said. "What's Homicide Special?"

"The LAPD's best of the best," he explained, remembering something he'd read a long time ago. "See, every LAPD bureau has its own set of homicide detec-tives, but whenever someone stands out, unlocks more than their share of cases, basically kicks ass and takes names, the heads of Homicide Special notice. So they recruit these detectives into their elite unit, and these are the guys who get the serious cases—the high-profile murders, the homicides or homicide attempts involving celebrities, the serial killings."

"Sounds charming," Emma replied. "So what does this have to do with us?"

"LAPD detectives wear casual dress." Joe leaned forward, pieces starting to click together in his head. "Those from Homicide Special wear suits. It's a way of distinguishing themselves, like the Army Ranger's black beret, back before it became part of the uniform for all Army personnel. Not that I'm bitter or anything."

"You were a Ranger?" At his nod, Emma continued. "And you think Rodriguez and Landau were from Homicide Special because they were wearing suits?"

"Yep."

"But we are not celebrities, nor have these events been particularly high-profile. Why would Homicide Special have any interest in this?"

Joe leaned back against the plush cushions of her couch and blew out a breath. That was the question, to be sure. Some pieces of this puzzle had fit together, but they had only served to show how large and gaping the hole in the center still was.

Her eyebrows drawing together in confusion, Emma shook her head, her gaze unfocused as she tried to comprehend what had just happened. "I've never been one to spew out literary quotes in everyday conversation like some of my peers, but something is definitely rotten in the state of Denmark." She looked up at him, worrying her bottom lip with her teeth. "How did you know about this Homicide Special?"

"Read an article once." An article that had practically jumped off the page at him, his instincts screaming about its importance. So he'd read the article, tore it out of the magazine and promptly buried it in a mound of papers inside his office filing cabinet.

"Emma," he said, "I'll make some calls, try to get to the bottom of this before I leave at the end of the week." His mind was whirring with details—where to go, who to talk to, what to ask. "In the meantime, try not to be alone right now. Don't walk around at night again, and keep your doors and windows locked at all times." He rose, and she followed suit, folding her willowy arms across her chest and rubbing her elbows. He didn't want her to be alone. He didn't want to leave.

"I thought you said the shooter wasn't after me?" she asked, just a touch of fear flickering in her bottle-green eyes.

"My guess is all this will stop once I go back to San Francisco, but I don't want you to take any chances." He walked around a large, antique chest that served as a coffee table. Emma followed. "Do you have someone who can come stay with you, or who will take you in?" he asked as they moved toward the front door. "Normally I'd offer to provide security, seeing as this is my fault, but I think it's best that I stay as far from you as possible."

She nodded. "My mother lives here, and I have friends who will help."

"Great."

When they reached the door, she held out her hand, and he shook it, feeling a moment of déjà vu as he recalled their last goodbye.

"Be careful, Joe."

"You, too. I mean it, Emma."

She licked her lips and started to say something, then stopped. He put his hand on the brass door handle.

"Something's unfinished here, Joe," Emma burst out. She pushed a handful of loose, golden-brown curls off her forehead with one graceful movement, causing them to move as if they were alive. "I know this is none of my business, but I think you need to stay. In L.A., I mean. Stay and finish this. Find out who's trying to hurt you."

He froze. Maybe she was right. Everything about his education and training was telling him to stay, to track down the person who had shot at him and put an innocent woman in danger just because she was in the wrong place at the wrong time. Stay and figure out why someone would want to hurt him, or them. Stay, and uncover the mysteries of his past, pull the black veil off the first few years of his life.

But every fiber of his being was screaming at him to leave. He didn't know much about where he came from, but he knew he hated L.A. and wanted to get out of here as fast as he could. And he also knew that some things were better left buried in the dark.

Close your eyes.

He pushed through the door, not allowing himself to look back at her, to feel any regrets. It was better this way. He'd stay sane this way. She'd be safer this way.

"Thanks, Emma Jensen Reese. I'll see you around." Bounding down the steps toward his Honda, Joe mentally calculated how long it would take him to change his airline ticket so he could leave this blasted city behind tonight.

"SO, HE'S GONE NOW?" Jane Jensen Reese rolled her chrome-and-steel wheelchair up to the kitchen table. She pulled her reading glasses off of her face, allowing them to dangle from the amber-and-amethyst eyeglass chain looped around her neck.

Emma adjusted her own pair of reading glasses on her nose and slid six Scrabble tiles from her wooden holder into her hand. "He said his plane leaves on Friday night."

With a deft flick of her wrist, she spilled the tiles on the table to spell S-P-O-N-D-E-E.

Jane smacked her palms on the table and snorted with disgust. "*Spondee.* What in heaven's name is a spondee?" She propped an elbow on the tabletop and wagged her finger at Emma. "You're making that up. You think that just because I didn't go to college that I don't know what's a word and what's not a word? That's not a word!"

"Mother, it is so," Emma responded matter-of-factly. Someone ought to film their Scrabble games sometime. Maybe watching herself behave like a child would shame Jane into playing like an adult. She could have sworn her mother cheated by switching out her unwanted letters when Emma wasn't looking. "Here. Look it up." Emma shoved her five-hundred-dollar, single-tome edition of the *Oxford English Dictionary* and its accompanying magnifying dome in her mother's direction. They'd had to put the extra leaf in the dining room table to accommodate that.

Jane flattened her mouth until the corners all but disappeared inside her apple cheeks. "It's a literary term, isn't it?"

Emma nodded.

"Oh, how I hate that." Jane sighed and drew four letters from the pile, concentrating intently on the maze of words before her. Jane, like Emma, took Tuesday night Scrabble very, very seriously. She flipped them into her holder and a slow smile spread across her face. "Ha!" she cried. "Ha. Ha. Hahahahaha." One by one, she snapped the wooden letters in place to lay I-M-P-A-S-T-O down from the *P* in Emma's *spondee*. "A painting term. I'll be Scrabble champion of the world yet. You just watch."

Emma snorted, but then looked up. "Your hair's crooked, Mom," she said, feeling a tenderness for her mother that made her chest ache as she tugged the shiny copper locks back into place.

Jane patted Emma's hand, the corners of her mouth turning up in a soft smile. "Thank you, dearest." She segued abruptly back to her original topic of the mysterious Joe Lopez, forcing the moment to pass. "At least we don't have to worry about strange men in fugue states lurking around your place. But truly, I'm surprised he's leaving."

Emma felt a pang of guilt at keeping secrets from Jane. She hadn't told—nor was she going to tell—her mother about the nighttime stalker or the shooting; her mom had enough to deal with.

"If he keeps coming to the house," Jane continued, "it means some part of his mind wants to remember. You have to wonder what could cause someone to lose memories of just a portion of their childhood?"

Just then, someone clumped through the door of Jane's two-bedroom La Brea apartment, and they both turned their heads at the noise. Celia gave them a cheery wave.

"Psychogenic amnesia," Celia said as she walked into the kitchenette, a chocolate pie with a single candle in the center in her hands. "Emma, after you called me, I looked it up on the Internet." She opened the refrigerator door to put the pie inside. "Most likely caused by major trauma he experienced as a child—*way* major trauma—" she spun around, the flared cuffs of her black-and-gray silk shirt swinging with the movement "—which caused him to block out all the memories of the event, and, from what he told you, the entire first ten years of his life. Consciously, he has no clue why he can't remember things, and he may even be curious about what is drawing him to your house. But every last neuron making up his unconscious mind is fighting to keep those memories repressed." Celia grabbed an apple out of the fruit bowl on the counter and crunched into it.

"You got all that from the Internet?" Emma asked.

Celia swallowed and shot her a toothy grin. "In my next life, I want to be a detective. There's no excitement in library science." She waved her apple at the dictionary on the table. "Except maybe when the *OED* publishes an updated edition."

Emma drew a handful of letters and spilled them out on the table before her, arranging and rearranging them with the pad of one finger. "It's true—he doesn't want to know. I could feel it. Even without the giant in-your-face hint he gave me by practically leaping into his car and leaving rubber tire tracks in the road." She built a very lame Q-U-I-Z off of the word *zephyr* on the board. "And really, it doesn't matter. He's gone now, and everything's back to normal."

She thought she heard her mother mutter something like, "That's what I'm afraid of," but before she could confront her about the statement, they were distracted by Celia taking her place at the table. They'd been doing Tuesday nights together for so long, they had the routine down pat.

"Happy birthday, Emma," Celia said, marking the only difference between tonight's get-together and the hundreds before it.

"Speaking of ruts," Jane said, returning to their conversation, "there's something I need to discuss with you." She picked up the board, folded it into a shallow *V* shape, and let the letters slide down the middle and back into the box—a clear sign that the game was over. "You were winning anyway, dear," she said in response to Emma's surprised squeak. "I want your full attention on this conversation. It's important."

Jane wheeled around, Scrabble box in hand. "I'm going to New Mexico tomorrow. For a month." She opened a cabinet drawer and tucked the game inside.

"Mom, midterm break is five weeks away," she explained patiently, folding her hands under her chin to support it. "You know I can't get away right now."

Jane spun back to face her, the fiery look in her green eyes reminding Emma for just a moment of the mother she'd once been, rather than the fragile woman whose hair Emma had held back while she vomited her guts out, or whose skin had grown so thin at one time that when Emma held her hand, it felt like paper.

"Why, Emma, dear, you're not invited."

"Not—?" Emma stood and pushed her chair back from the table in one abrupt movement. "What do you mean?" Celia came over and put her hand on Emma's shoulder. Emma turned to her friend, the beached-fish feeling from this afternoon coming back. "What does she mean?"

"She has an art show in Taos, Em," Celia said. "You should see her new stuff. It's really incredible."

"You can't!"

"I can." Even in her chair, Jane looked ten feet tall, and Emma felt like an awkward teenager tripping over her words.

"It's not safe."

"The Montero Gallery in Taos wants to hold a big show to launch my new paintings, and I'm going to be there," Jane boomed, and then her face softened. "Honey, you don't need to worry about me."

"Just a few weeks, Mom, and then I can go with you." Emma heard and hated the pleading note in her voice. It always meant that whatever she and her mother were arguing about, she would lose.

"The opening is next week," Jane said firmly.

"What about your doctor's appointment?"

"I've arranged to see a colleague of Dr. Stenson's in Taos instead."

"What about your pills?" Emma always

made sure her mother took her medication during her afternoon visits.

Jane smiled tenderly at her. "I don't need reminders to take them."

"How are you going to get there?"

"I'm going with a friend. In an RV."

Emma rolled her eyes and humphed to show how much she trusted that friend, whoever she was.

"Emmmmmaaaaa," Jane said, her voice pitched low with warning. "You are being unreasonable."

"Mother, you have cancer!" Choking on the word, Emma stalked past the two women and reached for the cutting board by the sink while pulling a carrot out of a nearby bowl. Her vision blurred.

"Yes, I *had* cancer. But that doesn't mean I'm going to sit around here and twiddle my thumbs while you act like a one-woman funeral procession before the doctor even tells me whether I'm dying or not."

Emma grimaced, unable to stomach the D word. Jane had been diagnosed with a cancerous tumor on her spine when Emma was ten, a few months after her mother and father had gotten the most amicable divorce in legal history. The end result was a long, torturous recovery that had culminated with an operation that took away the use of her legs. But her mother had grown strong again, and through the years, Emma had deceived herself that the cancer would never come back. And then, eleven months ago, it had, and she was scared beyond belief that the critical one-year checkup wouldn't end with the cheery, cancer-free prognosis her mother obviously expected. "You know as well as I do that you're not in the clear until the year is over," Emma said, swiping at her eyes with the back of the hand holding the carrot. She sensed Jane wheel up behind her and felt the pressure of her mother's hands as she stroked the small of Emma's back.

"It's going to be all right, sweetie," Jane said softly.

"It's not!" Emma whirled to face her. "Who's going to cook you dinner? Who's going to remind you to take your medication?"

"I will." Jane responded. "Or Ed will."

"Ed?" Celia and Emma blurted simultaneously.

"Ed Cavendish," Jane said. "We're driving down to Taos in his RV."

Emma turned back toward the counter and whacked the top off the carrot she'd been holding with a loud thunk. "And who, pray tell, is Ed Cavendish?"

Jane narrowed her eyes. "A very nice man I met at the Getty Museum."

Emma waved the knife while she searched for the right words to express her utter shock at the news that her mother was going to run off with some strange man. "How long ago? Do you know anything about him? What if he's a con artist? What if he has a police record?" She stabbed the air with each syllable. "You can't just go gallivanting across the country like that at a moment's notice. And in an RV, no less!"

Celia reached over and deftly plucked the knife out of Emma's too-expressive hand. Emma barely glanced at her. "Did you know most of those things run on diesel? Diesel!"

"Emma, I've known Ed's sister practically forever. We've both done shows at

Gallery 825. He's a nice man," Jane explained patiently.

"Oh, sure. Go ahead. Run off with some weirdo you just met and tear your own personal hole in the ozone. See what I care." She spun around to continue peeling the carrot, only to remember that the knife was no longer in her possession. So she just stood there, carrot in hand, and tried to make her once-again-blurry vision clear.

"Sweetheart." Jane wheeled behind her and put a hand on her back, rubbing her palm in gentle, soothing circles. "It's time for me to live again. And more importantly, it's time for you to live again."

Emma swiped at her eyes with the back of her hand and opened her mouth in protest. Jane cut her off. "Ever since the diagnosis, you've been doing nothing but working, sleeping, and taking care of me."

"Mom," she said, her voice breaking, "you almost died."

"And I promise, I'll try to avoid doing it again for as long as possible. But you can't put me in a pumpkin shell and refuse to let me live because of a stupid disease." Jane ran her hand along the back of Emma's arm until she reached her hand, which she grasped tightly. "I am so grateful for every moment you gave to take care of me while I was sick, but I've been your excuse for far too long. Trust me, this is going to be the best month of your life."

Emma jerked backward at the words.

"Baby, I know." Jane held on to her fingers more tightly. "I can't promise you everything's going to be all right, but even if it isn't, I want us to go back to normal. And that means I'm going to gallivant to Taos, and you're going to find your way again."

Celia moved behind Emma and put her hands on her arms, leaning her chin on one of Emma's shoulders. "And I'm here when you need me, Emma," she said.

The three of them stood quietly in Jane's kitchen, and Emma could feel herself shaking. It had been over two decades since her mother's first battle with cancer. If anyone had what it took to beat the disease twice in a lifetime, it was Jane Jensen Reese. But the thought didn't make her any less terrified. Jane and Celia were all the family she had, and to lose one of them would be too horrible to contemplate.

"Just for the record, it's not going to be the best month of my life." She let herself lean on Celia and felt her mother's embrace, stronger than it had been in a long time. "This really sucks, you know?" she said through her tears.

She heard her mother laugh softly behind her. "That's my girl."

Chapter Five

It had been more than twelve hours since Jane had left with Ed Cavendish, who, Emma had to admit, was a pretty charming guy. But Jane's grand adventure had left her with a giant ball of worry just under her ribcage and little to do with her free time. Her afternoon routine was shot; she'd spent so long taking care of and checking up on her mother than she hadn't a clue what to do with the hours that stretched before her after the last term paper of the day had a grade on it. She tried reading, watching movies, taking hot baths, even doing a Pilates DVD, but it all left her with a vague sense of unease, as if something in her day wasn't quite finished.

Too bad Joe Lopez hadn't fugue-stated

his way into her yard lately. At least it would have given her something to do.

Tugging her reading glasses off her face, she tucked them into their case and slipped them into her satchel. For the umpteenth time, she straightened the stack of student papers on her desk, then finally rose. Maybe she'd go visit Celia before she went home, see if the library had gotten in any new fiction—or maybe she'd revisit a favorite classic.

Five minutes later, she was in the stacks of the St. Thomas More Library, scanning the shelves from Hunter S. Thompson to Mark Twain and feeling unsatisfied with those books and, to tell the truth, everything else in the stupid, underfunded library. Not that Celia didn't work miracles with her small budget, but jeez. Could the lousy football team maybe do without a few hot tubs one year so the university could actually direct some money toward academic scholarship?

Emma shot a guilty glance toward Celia's office, where her friend was busy talking on the phone while flipping through the *Reader's Guide to Periodical Literature,* presumably answering a question for a student burning the 9 p.m. oil. The library was fine—more than fine for a small liberal arts university. They had a reciprocity agreement with the University of Southern California library, so it wasn't as if the resources of a larger school weren't easily accessible.

So what was her problem, then?

"Okay, Ms. Crabby Pants," she muttered to herself as she stalked back through the stacks. "Fiction isn't doing it. Let's find another distraction."

I don't remember the first ten years of my life.

"One that's not you, Joe Lopez." The memory came unbidden into her head, and once there, she couldn't shake it. Which really wasn't fair, since it was *his* unfinished business that was playing like a broken record inside her mind. It should have been haunting him, not making her wander the stacks instead of going home to a book and a bubble bath.

It's right here, but I can't see it.

"You don't want to see it," she said matter-of-factly, causing a young woman hard at work in a study carrel to peer at her over red plastic glasses. Emma widened her eyes and pursed her lips slightly—her scary professor face, Celia called it—and the girl ducked back behind her textbook.

What am I doing? she wondered, heading past the carrels to the magazine racks in the back. Some head case—some cute head case—wanders into her life, gets her stalked, gets her shot at, scares her to pieces and makes it *quite* clear he wants nothing to do with her, her house or her beloved city ever again, and she can't let it go? How sad. How pathetic. Just how the official, thirty-five-which-is-almost-forty-year-old Reese Family Spinster was supposed to act.

But here she was, she thought, staring at the microfilm machines against the wall, not letting it go.

Just a few minutes. Just to see if she could find anything. What the hey—she was bored anyway. Her gaze traveled from the machines to the adjacent shelves filled with heavy bound indices to the *Los Angeles Times*. Guesstimating Joe's age as being around the same as hers, she hauled a few volumes from the later 1970s to a nearby table and spread them out. The reading glasses went back on, and she went to work, looking for articles that mentioned her neighborhood, even her address, and some kind of significant event.

So Joe had suffered some trauma at age ten that had made him block out the first few years of his life. And someone was trying to kill Joe after learning through that fateful NAPI front-page article that he'd returned to the city. Therefore, it stood to reason that someone wanted something that was buried deep in Joe's broken memory left buried—some kind of crime that he'd witnessed, perhaps?

Emma drummed the fingers of her left hand on the table. A robbery? Wouldn't have traumatized a small child like that. Abuse? A possibility, but, although she was no psychologist, it seemed to her that Joe would have wiped out only the memories of the abuse and not the whole first decade of his life.

Murder?

A shudder caused her hand to clench the pencil it was holding. Dropping the pencil on the table, she grabbed a chunk of index pages and thunked them over to the left, which landed her in the *H*'s. Using her fingertip, she ran down the boldface cross-reference headings until she found Hancock Park, and then…

Nothing. At least in 1976. She repeated the procedure for 1977, then 1978.

And the abbreviated title her finger landed on in that volume had her running to the microfilm storage cabinets. She hauled open the drawer for June 1978, tugged the small box for June 12 out of its dust-coated spot and headed for the projectors. What she found once she'd threaded the film through the softly humming machine left her feeling clammy and light-headed.

LAPD's Daniela Lopez Shot Dead at Home. Cop Killer Still at Large.

Under the front-page headline was a headshot of a serious-looking though beautiful police officer. Even in black and white, Emma could see hints of Joe in Daniela Lopez's light eyes and glossy black hair. She skimmed the article and, unable to believe what she was reading, skimmed it again from the top once she'd finished. Then she moved on to the next article.

After several trips back and forth between the storage cabinet, the microfilm projector and the attached printer, she hit Print for the last time, then leaned forward to rest her forehead against the glass monitor, feeling exhausted. She had to find Joe and right away, but dear Lord, how was she going to do this?

How did you tell a man who'd lost his past that his parents had been horribly murdered? How did you tell him they'd never found the person responsible?

Where did you find the words to inform him that when his mother had died, he'd been there, and he'd seen the whole thing?

JOE WAS JUST FOLDING UP the last of his clothes and putting them in his suitcase— because halle-freaking-lujah, he was going home tomorrow, having resisted the urge to leave the conference early—when he heard a knock at the door.

He didn't like the sound of that knock.

Maybe that no-aim Sinatra freak was back, wanting to finish the job he'd botched so badly at Emma Jensen Reese's house. Maybe he didn't believe that Joe was just going to take his shiny little award and go back to San Francisco with a song on his lips and the best miniature bottle of cheap liquor he could buy on Southwest Airlines in his gullet. Maybe the confrontation Joe had been both anticipating and dreading was about to finally happen.

But really, would the dude knock?

Wearing only a pair of faded jeans and some droplets of water on his bare chest from a recent shower, Joe grabbed his gun off one of the nightstands and flattened his body against the wall next to the hinged side of the door. "Who is it?" he shouted.

The response jolted him away from the wall. He peered through the peephole, about five inches too low for him. And then he pulled open the door.

Sure enough, Emma Jensen Reese stood before him, wearing a black and off-white flowered dress with flowy sleeves. Where the dress stopped just above her knees, those ridiculous black boots with the giant heels continued, adding inches to her already formidable height. He wasn't used to women who could look him in the eye without craning their necks. She was curvier than the women he usually dated, too, but obviously he'd been missing out on something. Emma Jensen Reese had the kind of Amazon hourglass body a man could—

"Uh, Joe?" She narrowed her fearless green eyes at him, as if she'd been reading his mind.

Crap. He blinked. "Yeah, uh, hey. Can you hold on a second? I'm just going to put a shirt on." At her nod, he closed the door and drew a navy blue T-shirt over his head, ran some gel through his damp, tousled hair, and then opened the door again. "Come on in." He stepped back and waved her inside.

She came in and looked around. Fortunately, the room wasn't as much of a pit as it had been before he'd started packing. There was a small pile of clothes sitting next to his suitcase, but other than that, everything was pretty much shipshape.

But it wasn't the pile of clothes that made her uneasy. One quick glance revealed that the only place to sit in the tiny room was the bed—no table and chairs or desk like the bigger suites had. His San Francisco agency did well enough, but that didn't mean he didn't have to cut corners where he could—like not paying the fee to change his plane ticket so he could leave L.A. a few days early like a big girlie-man. All the more money to buy big electronic toys and king-size biscuits for Roadkill.

Emma bent to sit at the edge of the bed, then straightened again. *Awkward.* "You know—"

"There's a coffee shop downstairs. You feel like—"

She shot him a grateful look. "Actually, how about the bar?"

Her request startled him, and by the look on her face, startled her even more.

"*Ooo*kay," he said. She had a reason for

being here, he knew, and if she felt she needed some liquid courage to get her through the evening, maybe it wasn't a reason he'd like. Maybe he should just slam the door shut behind her and head for the airport early.

But he didn't listen to his gut, instead choosing to walk beside her to the elevator and into the hotel bar in companionable silence. The bar was done in an ocean theme, with a wave pattern painted on the walls, blue tables with what looked like aquarium rocks embedded in their tops, and a large fiberglass hammerhead shark hanging over the circular bar in the center of the large room. The lighting made every surface look as if water were rippling across it, giving the patrons, the staff and a lone woman selling roses out of a basket an otherworldly look.

Once Joe and Emma had seated themselves at a table for two in a less ripply corner, Joe folded his arms on the tabletop and leaned forward. "Emma, something's bothering you. What's up?"

"Just a second." She flagged the waiter and ordered a glass of Pinot Grigio.

He ordered a Stoli and Seven and waited for her to tell him what was on her mind. Which was delayed while she busied herself with a small string dangling from her flared sleeve, obviously stalling. He watched the weird lighting dapple her skin with blue and green wave patterns until the drinks arrived a few minutes later. She grasped her glass as if she'd just trekked across Death Valley, a grateful look on her pretty oval face. She took a sip of her wine. And then another. And another. And finally she just chugged the whole thing down as if it were a can of Bud Light with a hole punched in the bottom.

"Good wine," she gasped when she was finished.

"I can tell." Well, well. Ms. Elegance-is-My-Middle-Name could bolt 'em down with the best bar rats. Interesting.

Fingering the thin stem of her glass, she took a deep breath, blew it out through her full lips, and then looked him square in the eye with an intensity that threw him for a minute. "So," she finally began in that smoky voice of hers, making him think she'd fit right in if she started crawling on the baby grand in the corner of the bar and singing jazz, "working on a university campus, I have access to all sorts of research resources."

She paused; he waited. When she didn't continue, choosing instead to fidget with her glass and then the salt shaker, he raised his eyebrows at her. "And?"

"And—" abandoning the shaker, Emma rubbed her fingers in circular motions around her temples as if she had the mother of all headaches "—I know it wasn't any of my business, but I just couldn't let it go, you know, your connection to my house, your past, this creep who's trying to hurt you. Or me. Or whoever. So, I—" She swallowed.

"You dug something up on my past."

She blinked, but otherwise kept her surprise under wraps. He understood her reaction—male intuition was an oxymoron to most people. It was also a prerequisite for a missing persons detective.

"Joe," she said, folding her hands on the table and leaning toward him, the disco lighting making the moment even more surreal, "I dug everything up."

It took him a minute to let that sink in. "Everything?"

Her hands flew into the air, palms up, showing she was at a loss for how to continue, but then she got her bearings. "Not every moment of the ten missing years, of course. The big pieces." Swallowing, she continued. "I think I know why you chose to forget your childhood."

He did the only thing he could do upon hearing that little piece of news. He bolted.

PUSHING PAST PEOPLE, bellhops, and one old lady carrying a trembling, ancient poodle, Joe tore through the lobby and burst through the revolving doors at the front of the hotel, stopping once he was outside in the fresh air. Cars zoomed down the street, lined with impossibly tall, thin palm trees with brushy green tops that waved in the breeze. The sun had just started to go down, so brilliant orange, purple and red fingers trailed across the sky, made brighter by L.A.'s infamous smog. Joe scrubbed a hand across his eyes, as emotions so black and ugly they didn't have a name bubbled to the surface of his mind.

Who did she think she was, freaking earth mother to the free world? Digging around in his past as if she knew what was best for him. And without his permission. *He* was supposed to control this. His past was supposed to come to him when he was ready to face it. Or, if someone had to do some digging, it should have been him. Anger and resentment and, he could barely admit it, sheer panic swirled around in his gut, warring for dominance. He clenched his hands, digging his short nails into his palms.

Turn your head, baby.

He did *not* want to know what that dream meant. Or, at least, the few pieces of it he could remember when he woke.

Damn her.

And damn him for being a coward.

Feeling helpless and more than a little stupid, he looked around, wondering what to do with himself until he spotted a bench a few feet down the street. He strode to it and planted his hands on the backrest, watching—but not really watching—the cars go by.

She'd found everything.

Just as quickly as the anger and the panic had come, they were gone, and all he felt in their place was a silent, gray sorrow. For Emma, who'd cared enough to give him the gift of her concern and her time, only to have it thrown back in her face. And for his family, because he now knew, had always known, really, that something terrible had happened to them. Now there was no more running from it—no matter how many memories his subconscious blocked, it would only take a few seconds to bring himself face to face with the ugly truth.

He wondered how much it would hurt, to open up the manila envelope he'd seen resting at Emma's feet. There it had been, ten missing years of his life, the key to his past, all wrapped up inside one stupid little envelope, ready to explode around him like a Molotov cocktail. And at this moment, he knew he could just give the papers back to her, turn around and walk away. Forget L.A., forget the neat packet she'd assembled like some female Dudley Do-Right, forget everything but the life he'd built for himself after an adolescence spent in foster care and solitude.

But he could no more walk away than he could stop breathing. It was there. He hadn't searched for it, and he wasn't proud of that fact, but it was all there, and dammit, he was going to walk back into that hotel, open that envelope and take it like the man he'd become.

EMMA KNEW SHE'D GONE TOO FAR as soon as she'd seen the look in Joe's eyes when she'd told him she'd dug up his past. Stupid, stupid woman, she berated herself. Obviously she'd gone too far, and anyone would have known that well in advance except for her, Ms. I-Have-To-Prove-How-Smart-And-Resourceful-I-Am.

Beckoning the waiter with a polite smile plastered to her face, she ordered another glass of Pinot Grigio, this time sipping the wine instead of slugging it while she lost herself in her thoughts. After all she'd found out about Joe and his family, she'd felt from the very core of her being that it was best that he knew. But honestly, if the man's subconscious was working overtime to block out his entire childhood, you'd think she would have taken that as a huge clue that maybe he wasn't ready to face his past. And now she'd hurt him, and the tenuous beginnings of friendship she'd felt growing between them—and even the something more that might have been just her imagination, or might not—had snapped like overburdened bridge cables.

Twisting the fine stem between her fingers, she stared at the bottom of the glass as the remaining drops of wine swirled slowly around and around.

Just then, a red rose dropped onto the table. She lifted her head to tell the gift giver that she wasn't even remotely interested, even if he was the reincarnation of Gregory Peck himself, when she met a pair of familiar, whiskey-colored eyes. "Joe."

He sat down across from her once more,

slinging his leather jacket over the back of the chair. He leaned back with a deceptively easy, loose-limbed grace. To anyone else in the bar, he'd look relaxed, but facing him as she was, she couldn't ignore the explosive emotions swirling in his eyes.

"Look," he said quietly, "I'm sorry about that. I just needed a minute."

Emma shook her head, fingering the dethorned stem of the beautiful red rose he'd given her. "I wouldn't have blamed you if you'd gone back to your hotel room, never to darken my door again. It wasn't my place to dig around your past, but I had the means and I thought I could help. I won't blame you if you hate me for this."

He leaned forward, his dark hair falling across his forehead, and practically pinned her to her chair with his otherworldly stare. "I don't hate you, Emma."

As soon as the words were out, she realized he'd meant them, and the emotional maelstrom she'd felt coming on evaporated. He leaned down and closed his hand around the envelope at her feet, his fingers brushing hers when she instinctively tried to take it back from him. Once he had it on the table, he flipped it over to reveal the flap, which had been glued shut under the metal clasp. He went for the clasp, and she put her hand on top of his, stopping him.

"The articles I found on you are in there," she said softly. "Just say the word, and I'll put this away somewhere where you won't be able to find it unless you ask me." Turning her head, she stared at some invisible speck on the flat blue carpeting, feeling a flush rise up her cheeks. She raked her hair back with one hand. "You still have a choice, Joe, even if it seems like I took it away from you."

"How bad is it?" he asked.

Her mouth flattened into a thin line, and she closed her eyes briefly. Then she met his gaze head-on once more.

"It's not good, Joe."

He simply gave her that half smile of his and inserted his thumb underneath the flap, tearing open the top with one quick movement. She moved her chair so she could sit next to him.

The piercing eyes of Officer Daniela Lopez were the first thing he saw.

"Mom." He'd mouthed the word, and she could see the certainty and the sadness flicker across his face. Then, just as quickly, his expression hardened, and he turned back to the article in his hands.

It was an obituary, which she'd purposefully put at the top of the stack, as it was the only piece in the bunch that wasn't a straightforward news article about the tragedy that had stolen his memories.

Friends and fellow officers gathered today to pay their respects to Officer Daniela Lopez of the Los Angeles Police Department. The recipient of two LAPD medals for bravery in the line of duty, Lopez had been with the West Bureau for seven years.

The article focused on everything good about his mother, which wasn't something she could say about the other pieces she'd collected that thickened the stack behind it.

He skimmed the obituary, which heralded Daniela's bravery, her devotion to her family, and only briefly mentioned her murder by an unknown assailant. And Emma waited for Joe to discover the news that she'd felt so strongly he needed to know now.

His eyes darted to the bottom of the page, and his jaw tightened with an audible click of his teeth. She knew which line he'd just read.

Lopez is survived by her four children, José, Daniel, Patricio and Sabrina.

"Holy mother of God," he said, sitting back hard in his chair. Then his eyes lost their focus, and he looked right through her into something from his past.

"I don't like you all alone here, Mama," he said, and Emma could feel the goose bumps rising on her forearms. "Not after what happened to Papi."

"Joe." She brushed her fingers against his bare arm in a tentative touch.

"No, Mama, I'm staying here with you." He shook his head, his eyes still unfocused, and she moved her hand to grip his fingers.

"I can't protect them, Mama. I'm staying here with you." His eyes flicked back and forth, watching something in his past that she couldn't see.

"Joe," she called, loud enough that people at the next table glanced over to see what was going on. She ignored them. "Joe, it's Emma."

At the sound of her name, he shook his head, gripping her hand as if he were a drowning man, so tightly that his knuckles had turned white and she could feel the pressure on her fingers. His chest rose and fell with his rapid breathing. "Emma," he said, a statement, not a question.

"I'm here."

"I need you to protect Sabrina, Patricio and Daniel."

She blinked, confused. Obviously he was still lost in some dreamland. "Joe, I don't—" Reaching out, Emma placed her hand on his arm, trying to bring him back from the insane whirlwind of tattered memories that seemed to threaten to engulf him and never let go, like a pack of mad poltergeists.

"It was one of the last things my mother said to me." He let go of her hand and laughed bitterly. "Some job I did. I lost them for over two decades."

"Lost—?"

"I have two brothers and a sister," he explained. "Sabrina, Patricio and Daniel."

Then Emma understood. Deep inside his mind, Joe still remembered them. And they, like him, had lived.

"They're out there, Joe," she said. "Somewhere, maybe even here in Los Angeles, you have a family."

Chapter Six

Emma inserted the key into the lock on her front door and pushed inside, trying not to dwell on the memory of Joe's face when he'd learned he'd had a family. A loving family that had been destroyed by the murder of his parents, just days apart.

And no one had ever been able to figure out who'd killed them or why they'd died.

It was sobering, really. After all, she'd always missed having a father, but to lose both parents at such a young age, and then to lose all memory of them and the siblings you once had? No wonder the guy had issues.

But now that she'd gone above and beyond the call of duty—and maybe even decency—and had filled in the missing pieces of Joe's past, it was time to let go.

He had still insisted on flying back to San Francisco tomorrow morning, and she was going to go back to her life. Jane was due back in three weeks, and Emma would need all her reserves to make it until that fateful doctor's appointment. She'd helped, he had his past tucked into the small envelope she'd given him, and now maybe he could heal and she could move…

A noise like a footfall sounded in the next room, near the main staircase.

Emma froze. She was almost in the doorway and could see part of the stairway through the opening. Slowly, softly, she set her cumbersome shoulder bag down on the hardwood floor and listened for another noise. Old houses like this often made odd noises as they "settled"—a phenomenon she was all too familiar with, having lived in this ten-bedroom behemoth for the last three years. So why did that one little noise have the hair on the back of her neck standing on end?

Unable to ignore the fact that every cell in her body was flashing WARNING!, she lifted her right foot, swung it slowly behind her left ankle and softly set the sole onto the floor, inch by careful inch. When that step backward turned out to be successfully quiet, she repeated it, keeping her eye on the stairs.

A shadow stepped out from behind her and solidified in the dim moonlight streaming through the leaded glass windows.

Emma swung around, prepared to make a run for it.

"I wouldn't do that if I were you," the shadow hissed. She heard the sound of a gun being cocked.

Her heart hammering in her ears, Emma slowly turned to face him. The intruder was dressed in black, a nylon stocking pulled over his face to obscure his features.

Oh, God, what was she supposed to do? The man was in her house, and unless she could beat him to the door, there was nothing and no one to stop him from doing whatever he wanted to her. Not to mention the man had a gun. She glanced around wildly for something, anything she could use to defend herself. It was futile. "What do you want?" she asked.

"To send a message," he whispered.

A message. Okay, he hadn't said, "To kill and dismember you and dispose of your body in a Dumpster," so cooperating might be the thing to do. She clenched her hands together, trying to control her sudden shaking.

He walked toward her, stopping when his mouth was close to her ear. Emma swallowed the reflexive gag response at his proximity and forced herself to remain still. "I didn't have to miss," he said, and she knew he was referring to the gunshots embedded in her siding. "Those were a warning, and here's your last one."

He paused; she waited. Finally, after what seemed like an eternity, during which every fiber of her being wanted to shriek her fool head off and bolt, he said, "Tell Detective Lopez to leave the city, or I'll kill him. I'd rather not wait, but you know how it is." He reached out to finger a lock of her hair. "And wouldn't it be too bad if pretty Professor Reese got in the way again?"

Emma jerked back, startled that he even knew her name.

With one hand still in her hair, he cupped her waist with the other and ran his face along her exposed neck. "The smell of fear on a beautiful woman. It's intoxicating."

He slipped something long and soft around her throat, and that's when she finally moved, jerking out of his grasp and flattening her body against an antique china cabinet. The hundred-year-old wood and glass rattled as her weight hit it. He let her go, laughing softly as he backed into the darkness behind the stairs.

It wasn't until she'd heard him slip out the window behind the stairs that Emma noticed he'd looped her missing scarf around her neck like a noose.

AS SOON AS JOE RECEIVED Emma's message, he borrowed a nondescript sedan from another conference attendee he had a passing acquaintance with and drove directly to her house. So much for avoiding his past—not only had it had come looking for him, it was leaving threatening messages with the one person in L.A. he'd considered a friend.

So, a short drive later, he parked a couple of blocks behind June Street and walked swiftly to Emma's back door, taking care to keep to the shadows. She answered seconds after his knock and let him inside.

All she'd told him was that she'd received a message from their friendly neighborhood shooter, but not what form the message had taken. One look at her pale, drawn face, and he knew it had been bad.

"Hey." She wrapped her hands around her elbows, hugging herself, but other than that and her too-serious expression, she looked completely composed. "Thanks for coming."

"No prob." He glanced around, assessing the entranceway. The windows he could see were still intact, and the front door hadn't shown any signs of a break-in, but as he recalled from their first afternoon together, it was the back door locks that needed a security update. Badly.

"I'm going to take a look around, see if I can't fix some of the less-secure areas of this house, and—" He took another look at Emma and stopped himself, dropping the few pieces of equipment he'd brought with him. No longer the Amazon who'd tried to pepper-spray him a few days ago, she looked small and very scared, though she was trying her best to hide it. "Ah, come here," he said softly. She came. Thank God.

He enfolded her in his arms and held her tightly, trying to give her some of the comfort she obviously needed. She was silent, with her arms tucked against his chest and her face burrowed in his neck, and he was hyperaware of her warm breath against his collarbone, her warm, curvy body against his. She wasn't crying, he noted with relief, but something had scared Emma Jensen Reese to pieces.

"Tell me about it," he said into her hair, not letting her go. So she told him, quietly and still without tears, and by the time she was finished, he knew he wasn't going to leave L.A. Friday, nonrefundable airline ticket be damned. He'd stay; he'd unearth his past, and he'd finish this once and for all, fix it so Emma could walk the streets and be in her house again without feeling she was in danger. He'd never once felt the urge to kill a living soul, but this guy was cutting it close.

"Damn, Emma, I'm sorry," he said, because he couldn't think of anything else to say.

She raised her head, reminding him just how tall she was. Her face was nearly level with his, and he was six-three. "For what?" she asked.

Ah, God, this was so not good. Because she was very good at making his darkest emotions just melt away like candle wax. And this time, he'd gone from his very first murderous impulse to very badly wanting to take the bottom lip Emma loved to chew on when she was worried into his own mouth, and then to kiss her until neither one of them could see straight.

He dipped his head, and damn if she didn't raise hers to meet it. But just as his lips brushed hers, he pulled back. Emma had had a nice life before he'd come along and brought his gun-toting, SUV-driving, one-maniac entourage into it. She was a lady in the truest, nonsexist sense of the word, and she didn't need the likes of him around.

"For dragging you into my messed-up life," he said, laughing. It sounded hollow even to his ears.

Before he could disengage himself from her, she leaned forward and kissed him on the cheek. Even that small contact made his nerve endings sing. "Not your fault," she whispered against his skin. "I had a birthday yesterday, and I wished for a grand adventure, just like I do every year."

The corners of his mouth quirked upward. "Confucius say, be careful what you wish for."

"Exactly." Then she was the one who pulled away, and her expression was sober. "Look, seriously, it's not your fault. That maniac is after you, and I just had the bad luck to buy and restore the broken-down house that holds the key to getting this homicidal monkey off your back." She gestured toward the open doorway to the liing room, which he'd avoided looking at since he'd goten there. "Come in, Joe.

Look around—being in here brought back some memories last time you did so. I want to help you get to the bottom of this. Because you're a hunted man until you do."

He took a deep breath and blew it out as he rubbed the suddenly tight muscles in the back of his neck. His earlier resolve to stay in L.A. and do just what she'd suggested now didn't seem like the best idea he'd ever had. "But if I go, he'll leave you alone. That's what he told you."

She shook her head. "I don't think so. He followed you to my house that first night. I'm sure he knows your memories are coming back. He'll follow you back to San Francisco, and he'll finish what he started when he killed your parents. And maybe he'll come back for me because I've seen him now, and I might know too much."

Joe swore under his breath.

Emma gripped his elbows and looked him dead in the eye with that stare of hers. "You know I have an inordinately high probability of being right."

"Oooh, out come the big words."

"Joe, stay in L.A.," she said, ignoring his

stab at mood-lightening sarcasm. "Finish this. And I think you should get the police involved."

He raked his hair off his forehead with one hand. "I talked to Rodriguez this morning who, by the way, is Homicide Special, just like I thought. Says he and his partner were the closest to your house when the call came in. They've been canvassing the neighborhood since the shooting, but no one saw anything."

She narrowed her eyes. "How old is Rodriguez? He's LAPD, and so were your parents. And he was acting strange when he was here."

"Not that old. I'd place him about five years younger than I am."

She snorted. "Couldn't tell with those goofy glasses he was wearing in the house. And it doesn't mean he isn't connected somehow to current events." Then she reached out and pulled one of her ornate dining room chairs away from the dark-stained table. "Tell me what you remember," she said suddenly, a clear invitation.

To his surprise, he didn't mind the personal question, feeling more comfortable around Emma than he had around anyone for as long as he could remember. Sure, he had friends back in San Francisco, but they were basketball-and-barbecue types who were good for a cold beer and a few laughs. Nothing deep. Certainly not Freudian "tell me about your childhood" conversations.

"Beth," he said before he could stop himself.

She blinked at him. "Who's Beth?"

"My second foster mother. My first was a nice lady, but she just didn't know what to do with me, you know?" He gestured for her to sit in the chair she'd pulled out and made himself comfortable across the table from her. "I don't remember much about the logistics surrounding how I got into the California foster care system, but I do remember how I felt. Lonely. Hollow. Lost. All these big feelings, and I couldn't remember why I was having them, couldn't answer anyone's questions about them or me. So I just stopped talking. And after a few months of radio silence, my first foster family gave up and tossed me back into the system, and it spat me out on Beth Billings' doorstep."

Emma rested her chin in one hand, listening intently. "I hope she was good to you."

He shook his head. "She was great to me. She took in the problem kids. You know, the ones who got into fights or got arrested for stealing or were labeled head cases, and she loved us to pieces. Simple as that. We would have rather cut off our own heads than disappoint Beth."

"She sounds amazing."

Joe nodded. "Yeah. So those are the last things I remember. Waking up one morning in the home of my first foster family, transitioning out, and then Beth." He got up, feeling a little weird at having told her more about his past in five sentences than anyone else. "What about you?"

Emma straightened her spine, shooting him a slightly bewildered look. "What about me?"

"Vhy don't you tell me about your childhood," he said in his best attempt at a fake German accent, which really wasn't so bad.

Relaxing once more, chin in hand, Emma shrugged. "Nothing much to tell. I'm an only child. I have great parents. They divorced when I was nine, but as befitting a couple who got married in Woodstock—the peace, love, and music Woodstock—it was the most amicable divorce ever. They became 'co-parents' and friends, and I never really missed having a conventional family."

"Cool," Joe said.

She pressed her finger down on a fleck of dust marring the shiny surface of the heavy oak table and then flicked it onto the floor. Then she told him about her mother's cancer, how it had nearly taken Jane from her when she was ten and how it had come back eleven months ago.

"Funny how the worst years of our lives happened to both of us when we were ten," she said, picking up more dust flecks, real and imaginary.

"I'm sorry," he said. "That sounds lame, but I mean it. That must have been really hard on you, then and now."

She smiled at him, then. "Not really. I can't imagine being in your shoes."

"I went looking for them today," Joe said abruptly. "My family," he supplied at Emma's puzzled look.

Emma straightened in her chair, interested. "What did you find?"

"Nada." He gave her a wry smile. "Would you believe the adoption records for all three of them were destroyed in a fire back in the eighties?"

She made a face. "Nothing about this can be easy, can it?"

He hitched a shoulder. "Guess not. But I'll find them. I work missing persons cases all the time." He wished he felt as confident as he sounded—without any records, finding Patricio, Daniel and Sabrina was going to take a hell of a lot of work. Then again, it wasn't as if he had anything better to do, other than hang around L.A. and get shot at.

Joe pushed away from the table and stood. "Look, it's late. I'm going to go through your house and make sure it's secure."

Standing herself, Emma flicked her gaze toward the living room door once more.

"I'm not avoiding the living room," he said.

"Of course not," she agreed, with no conviction whatsoever.

He picked up the hammer and nails and dead bolt set he'd brought with him and walked toward the living room. So if he was going to have one of those memory attacks in the house, he might as well get it over with.

He stalked into the doorway, his gaze taking in the sage-green overstuffed sofa, the oriental rug on the ground, the dark-stained antiques scattered about the room. And then…

Nothing.

The room, which the mere thought of entering had given him a severe case of vertigo, seemed vaguely familiar, but that was it. No passing out. No nightmare flashbacks. Nothing.

Huh.

He checked the window locks, then moved through the rest of the house, nailing the loose window behind the stairs shut and installing a new dead bolt on the back door for extra security. Then he went to the front door, uneasiness tugging at the corners of his mind. Emma shouldn't be alone tonight. But he sure as hell shouldn't be the one keeping her company, making her house a big target for that whistling perv.

He went to the front door, preparing to leave, then finally turned to face Emma, who had been silently following him as he checked the house. "Okay, what I've done will keep someone from entering silently, but you really ought to get a security system installed."

Emma glanced back at the stairs, obviously thinking about the man who had broken into her home. "Okay."

More than ever, he worried about her being alone. "Call me," he said impulsively. "If you just want me to check out a strange noise or something outside. I don't care if you think it's stupid—if the slightest thing makes you uneasy, just call me."

Tilting her head, she gazed at him for so long, he almost squirmed. "You're a really nice guy, Joe Lopez," she said.

"Yeah, whatever," he replied quickly. "Night, Emma."

"Good night, Joe."

As he made his way quickly around the house to the back alleys, he couldn't shake the feeling that someone was watching him, watching the house, watching Emma. And once again, he was struck through the core of his being with the stark certainty that she really shouldn't be alone tonight.

Chapter Seven

His mother's face floated into his line of vision, a pale oval framed by dark hair pulled back into a loose ponytail. The slight lines around her large, brown eyes crinkled with love and concern as she looked at him. They also held an unspoken message—he shouldn't have come.

She reached for him, brushing his hair away from his forehead with the softest of touches. "Close your eyes, José Javier," she whispered. He did.

He heard something slide back and then felt his mother's soft hands guiding him into an enclosed space. His eyes snapped open. "Mama, no!" he cried, struggling to push himself back into the living room.

"Shhhhh. It's okay, corazon," she whispered. "Stay quiet and be strong for me."

Something told him not to protest anymore. Maybe it was the sick feeling in his stomach or just the frightened look in his mother's eyes. With a gulp and a bravado he didn't feel, José nodded and did as he was told.

"Love you, baby," his mother said, touching his cheek before sliding the panel into place.

Tucked into the enclosed space, he could only listen in the darkness as his mother walked back into the living room. He heard voices, the sound of something heavy being knocked over, and then...a gunshot? Maybe his mother had turned on the TV.

But then he heard her cry out, heard another gunshot and then silence. A few seconds later, the only sounds he could hear were his hands beating against the closed panel door and his own screams.

THE BODYGUARD WATCHED Emma Jensen Reese peer through her bedroom curtains, unable to sleep on this balmy Southern

California night. Now she could have woken to appreciate the full moon that burst through the nighttime smog and overcame Los Angeles's light pollution, but he doubted it. After several days of watching her and her house, he knew better. She woke because Joe Lopez was watching her.

And he was watching Joe Lopez.

Lopez had been a challenge. He moved through the city like the north wind, blowing first one way, and then another, impossible to see, impossible to follow. But eventually, inexorably, something drew Lopez back to the house where his parents had died, like a moth to a spider's web. So all the bodyguard had to do was wait, like the spider.

Unfortunately, his employer also preferred watching and waiting to taking action, so Joe Lopez was still alive, despite the laughable number of opportunities the bodyguard had had to eliminate him. But it was only a matter of time. His employer thought Joe would leave the city, would leave the dead buried, along with their secrets.

The bodyguard knew better. The same

thing that kept drawing Joe to his childhood home was probing his mind, opening it up to flashes of memory that might, eventually, prove to be the trail of breadcrumbs that would lead him to the bodyguard and his employer. And they couldn't have that. His employer would eventually realize that.

Amnesia didn't last forever.

Fortunately, death did.

And then, while the bodyguard was cleaning up loose ends, he'd take his time with Joe's pretty girlfriend, Professor Emma Jensen Reese. She'd be his reward. And then she'd just be another loose end that had been all cleaned up.

Pretty Emma. Pretty, pretty Emma.

UNABLE TO SLEEP, Emma padded across the frayed kilim carpet on her bedroom floor and sat down on the Victorian chaise in front of the window overlooking the street. She'd gone downstairs to the kitchen earlier for a cup of hot cocoa, but so far it hadn't helped her insomnia. Toying with the still-warm mug in her hands, she peered through a small opening in the curtain at the street below.

A slight movement by one of the cars parked across from her house caught her eye, making the hair on the back of her neck prickle. Not again. He wouldn't come back twice in one night, would he?

Carefully placing the mug on the floor, Emma glanced at the nightstand where her bedroom telephone lay, along with her rarely used but fully charged cell phone. Secure in the knowledge that she could call the police in seconds, she gripped the back of the chaise and stared intently through the curtain.

The movement had come from inside a dark-colored but otherwise nondescript sedan. She zeroed her attention on it, noting that the lumpy shadow on the driver's side could be a person.

In a matter of seconds, her theory was proven correct as the lump stretched his or her arms up to the car's ceiling, then slouched back down again.

Well. What do we do now?

She was about to slip off the chaise and

call the police or Joe or *someone,* when the sedan's door opened, and a male figure stepped out if it. He looked quickly up and down the street, and as the moonlight illuminated the prominent features of his face, Emma knew exactly who'd been watching her front door that night.

Joe.

Unbelievable. She'd recognize that hawk-like Aztec nose and striking profile anywhere. Emma had thought he'd gone beyond the call of duty after he'd come across town to check the locks on her doors and windows. She hadn't asked him to stay, and he hadn't even hinted that he was thinking about it, or she would have made him up a bed. It wasn't as if she didn't have ten bedrooms or anything...

After quickly shedding her nightgown, replacing it with a pair of black, straight-leg sweats and a red St. X T-shirt, Emma took one last glance at Joe, still standing next to his car, and made her way downstairs. If neither of them was getting any sleep, at least they could keep each other company. And she'd start the conversation by asking him what the bloody heck he was doing going all Sir Lancelot in the middle of her street and putting a big fat target on his forehead in the process.

"Men," she muttered, undoing the locks and then opening the front door.

A large body filled the doorway. With a yelp, she nearly slammed the door shut again, until she realized a split second later that Joe had apparently migrated from the road to her front steps.

"Joe?" Something about him wasn't quite right. His eyes were glazed, and he was staring right through her, like a *Night of the Living Dead* zombie. She waved a hand in front of his face, then snapped her fingers under his nose when that failed to elicit a response. "Joe? Earth to you."

Unfortunately, her efforts still hadn't made a difference. The man continued to hover in her doorway without acknowledging her presence or even *blinking,* and he was starting to seriously creep her out. Maybe the shooter had already gotten to him. Maybe he'd injected Joe with some of that voodoo powder she'd read about that made you act like a zombie until it wore off. Maybe—

"Excuse me," Joe muttered as he gently gripped her elbows and moved her out of his way.

You wouldn't think that a few hours of sleep deprivation would make her think like a crazy woman, but apparently it did. Voodoo powder. Jeez.

Emma closed and locked the door, then followed Joe, who moved like a sleepwalker through her front sitting room and parlor, past the staircase and into the hallway that ran to the back of the house. Pausing at the doorways on either side of the hallway—one that went to the living room and one that went to the library—Joe turned left without hesitation into the room he'd mostly been avoiding all this time.

When she caught up to him, he was pounding softly with closed fists on the north wall, the one that adjoined the formal dining room toward the back half of the house. She felt along the wall until her fingers connected with the light switch. Soft light from her handmade beaded table lamp and the Dale Tiffany glass she'd gotten at auction flooded the room.

"Let me out," he said, and she could see that his gold-colored eyes still had that faraway look to them.

"Joe," she called softly, wondering if there was any truth to the old adage that waking a sleepwalker was dangerous. "You're dreaming, Joe. Wake up."

He pounded harder. "Somebody, let me out." Soon, his fists were beating against the pale yellow walls, causing her cheap art reproduction posters to rattle in their expensive glass frames. "Let me out of here!

Oh, God. "Joe." Emma propelled herself forward, trying to catch Joe in her arms before he damaged his hands. One of her frames went crashing to the floor in a pile of shattered glass and splintered wood, but she didn't care. "Joe, please, wake up." He struggled against her, but she held on, smoothing his hair and whispering soothing words in his ear. "It's me. Shhhh, it's Emma." He pulled away from her, but she came right back, placing her hands on his shoulders. "Please, wake up. You're not locked in anywhere anymore."

Just when she thought his efforts to get away from her might throw her against the wall, he stopped, his breathing ragged. "Get the hell away from her," he growled.

"I'm not anywhere near her," she said. "Come back, Joe. It's Emma." She took his beautiful face in both of her hands. "Look at me. It's Emma."

Before she could stop herself, Emma impulsively leaned forward and kissed him softly on the forehead. "Come back," she breathed against his skin.

She felt him relax in her hands.

"Emma?" He blinked, shook his head, then reached up to wrap his hands around her wrists, and finally, finally, he focused on her face. "Emma, what happened? What did I do?"

"Had the scariest sleepwalking moment of the year, I think," she said. Her hands fell away from his face, and he let go of her wrists.

"No," he responded, still looking at her hands, a lock of hair falling into his eyes.

"I didn't fall asleep. I never fall asleep when I'm on surveillance."

She opened her mouth to berate him for putting her under said surveillance without bothering to tell her, but then stopped. That wasn't important right now. "Then what was that?"

Meeting her gaze once more, he shrugged. "No clue. One minute I was watching you look out your bedroom window, and the next thing I knew, I started remembering that night. It was the nightmare I've had all my life, but this time in sharper color and more detail, like I was watching a movie. I was awake, and I can still remember it, which isn't normal."

Guiding him to her sage-green sofa, Emma sat and pulled him down beside her. "What did you see?"

Leaning forward so that his elbows were resting on his knees, he scrubbed a hand across his face. "My mother. She was here, alone, waiting for someone after my father's death. We were…at a neighbor's, my brothers and I, with the baby."

Emma held her body perfectly still, not

wanting to even breathe if it meant interrupting the fragile memories that had recently resurfaced from the darkest parts of Joe's mind.

"I came back, wanting to protect her, but I don't know from what. Maybe from whatever it was that had killed my father?" He was speaking so softly, Emma had to lean in to hear him. "There was a door in here—small, like a panel. She opened it and tucked me inside."

Emma glanced around them, knowing as she did so that there was no door in the living room, other than the one to the hallway.

"It was dark in there," he continued. "And I couldn't see anything. I could just hear. Oh, God, her scream." He sat up and looked right at her then, his whiskey-colored eyes full of loss and a young boy's heartache. "She saved me," he said, his voice flat and toneless. "If I hadn't come home, she could have saved herself."

Not knowing what to say to that, to yet another horrible memory resurfacing in

Joe's consciousness, Emma simply put her arms around him and laid her head on his shoulder.

THE TWO OF THEM remained entwined on the couch, silent, until the first rays of morning sunlight filtered through the smog and then through the leaded glass windows of the old Victorian house. At some point, Emma had fallen asleep, one arm slung around his back, her cheek resting against his shoulder. A slight puddle of drool pooled on his shirt under her chin, and every once in a while, a soft, feminine snore erupted from her open rosebud mouth.

Slowly, gently, he moved her arm, tucking it against her stomach, then tipped her back so her head was resting against the crook of his arm. The steady rhythm of her breathing didn't change, and her head lolled back so her incredible hair cascaded down his arm. He let himself just look at her for a minute. Had he ever been able to sleep with such abandon?

Catching her behind her knees with his other arm, he finally rose and carried her through the house, back to the stairway and up the stairs. Since he'd seen her—or maybe just sensed her—looking at him through the filmy curtains of her window when he'd been in his car, he knew her bedroom was at the front of the house. So he hooked a right at the top of the staircase, and from there, it was easy to find.

He approached her bed, a four-poster with peach-colored sheets and more filmy curtains surrounding it, and laid her on top of it. With one truly incredible snort, she curled her arms against her body and rolled on her left side, her back to him. Her breathing evened out, and she was asleep once again.

Tucking a blanket around her, Joe almost leaned down and kissed her good-night. Almost. But now he knew that not only was he a head case, but he was a head case who had pretty much sent his own mother to her death. Not the kind of man a woman like Emma Jensen Reese needed in her life.

So what now, champ? Taking care to close the door behind him as quietly as he could, Joe made his way back down to the living room, where his discarded gun and shoulder holster lay on the coffee table. He could leave, but he'd be taking a gamble as to whether his unknown enemies would leave Emma alone once he did. He could stay and try his damnedest to protect her and find out who wanted him dead, but would it be enough? Could he keep her safe by himself? Because he knew no one in L.A., and none of his friends back home were the kind of security experts he'd require if he were to pull extra bodies in on this…thing. His agency was a one-man operation, so there'd be no help there. And the LAPD was stretched thin enough—he was pretty sure they weren't about to waste valuable officers on what to them probably looked like a one-time drive-by.

Basically, he was all she had.

"And she wouldn't even need you if you hadn't brought this mess to her door in the first place," he growled to himself.

So, he thought as he pulled on his shoulder holster and jacket and headed for the door, here are the rules: keep her safe, find out who this creep is and get him before he gets you.

Enough said.

With that, he stepped outside. Just as he was about to lock the door, he noticed the copy of the latest *L.A. Times* sitting on Emma's doorstep, neatly rolled up into a plastic-covered bundle, which he picked up and tossed inside. At that same moment, Emma's elderly neighbor—presumably the Mrs. Bernard who was mother to Louis—stepped outside her house to collect her own paper.

"Well, good morning!" she called.

"Er, good morning," he said, knowing exactly what it must look like, his leaving Emma's house at oh-dark-hundred in the morning.

"It's about time Emma had a nice young man come calling. I worry about her," Mrs. Bernard said, her frankness confirming his fears.

"I'm not—" Joe stopped himself. She'd believe what she wanted to believe.

Clutching the pink terry cloth lapels of her bathrobe, the woman bent to retrieve her newspaper, slipping it out of the plastic. "Sorry to scare you." She ran her fingers through her tumbled gray curls. "No one's usually out and about at this hour."

"You didn't scare me at all, Mrs. Bernard." Joe paused, squinting at her in the early morning sunlight. She looked a little disheveled, as did anyone who'd just woken up. But that wasn't what he was looking at. What he really wanted to know was whether Mrs. Bernard had lived in that house for a long time—whether she'd known his family when they'd been in the home next to hers. Because time had stopped when she'd walked outside, and every cell in his body was telling him this moment was more than a mere exchange of pleasantries. "It is Mrs. Bernard, right?"

"So polite." She beamed at him. "Yes, it is. Call me Jasmine, though."

Go back to Jasmine's and take care of your brothers and sister.

It was like a splash of cold water to the face, but he caught his breath, schooled his expression and did his level best to look charming despite the fact that he generally didn't do charming at 5 a.m. Basically, he didn't even do marginally polite until after at least a vat of coffee. But this was important—maybe more important than anything in his life so far. With anticipation making his chest feel as if it would explode, he stepped off the front stoop of Emma's house, walking through the grass until he reached Mrs. Bernard's property line. He knew he'd never forget this moment if he lived to be a hundred. "I hope this doesn't seem nosy to you, ma'am, but have you lived here long?"

"All my life," she responded, her words kick-starting Joe's pulse into overdrive. She moved down three steps until she also stood on the grass. "This house used to belong to my parents, and—" She inhaled sharply and pressed a hand to her terry cloth-covered collarbone. "As I live and breathe."

He waited, his heartbeat nearly drowning out her words.

Peering intently at his face, Mrs. Bernard padded in her fuzzy pink slippers through the yard until she stood toe-to-toe with him, her riotous curls bouncing with the movement. "Normally I wouldn't get this close to a handsome young man unless I had my face on, but my goodness." The hand on her upper chest moved up to cradle her papery cheek. "You're a Lopez, aren't you?"

He felt the rest of the world slip away, until he was aware only of himself, Jasmine Bernard and the patch of grass they were standing on. "How did you know?"

The corners of her mouth turned up in a wistful smile. "You boys used to play with my Louis, and you were so kind to him, even with his mental state and all. And all of you had those intense, golden-colored eyes, like three little baby hawks. I figured there can't be too many men running around with eyes like that, especially in this neighborhood." She covered her mouth for a moment, her eyes growing watery, and then she opened her arms. "May I?" she asked, then stepped forward and clutched him in a remarkably strong hug for such a tiny, elderly woman.

She smelled of lavender sachets, he

thought, and then was struck by the fact that he had no recollection of having smelled lavender, or even of knowing what exactly a sachet was. He hugged her back. It felt familiar.

When she finally pulled away, she was laughing and swiping at her cheeks. "My goodness, I'm a mess." She cupped his face with both of her small hands. "Which one are you? If I had to guess, I'd say José Javier."

He nodded, not daring to speak.

"After your poor mama—" She stopped herself. "Well, I never knew what happened to you all and that sweet baby girl. It means the world to me to see you looking so well. How are your brothers?"

Turning his head, Joe gazed at the street, which was just starting to wake up. A couple of cars breezed by, a Volkswagen Beetle convertible and a Mercedes, and further down the street, a couple of dogs were having a bark-off. "I'm not sure, Mrs. Bernard." He shoved his hands into his pockets and looked at her once more.

Her mouth twisted, making the lines

around her lips stand out. "I don't understand."

Inhaling deeply, Joe plunged right in. Better to rip the bandage off quickly than peel it off slowly and prolong the hurt. "My memories of my family, this place... they're gone. They've been gone for a long time."

She frowned slightly, reaching out to rub his arm in a grandmotherly way. "Now that I can certainly understand. What do you remember?"

He paused for a moment. "I know Joe Lopez is my real name. I know I've spoken both English and Spanish since I was a child—I think my family was Mexican and Honduran. I know my parents are dead. That's all I've known until this week, when I found out that I had siblings and that I watched my mother die."

"Oh, you poor boy." She pressed her hands to her cheeks once more. "They separated you?"

"Yeah."

She tilted her chin upward, a resolute look in her eyes. "Can you come inside?" she asked abruptly. "Give me a minute to tame this mop, and then we can talk. I want to know how you've been after all this time." She reached her hands up in a futile attempt to smooth her crazy hair. "And how I can help."

"Sure, ma'am. I'd like that." And he realized he would. It wasn't just the information she could provide him, which would probably be considerable once he told her about his little memory lapse, but there was something about her that resonated somewhere. She made him feel like he'd come home.

EMMA WOKE TO FIND herself in bed, still in yesterday's sweats and red T-shirt, with a light blanket covering her and her shoes lined up neatly next to the bed, rather than still on her feet as they had been when she'd fallen asleep. A quick search through the house told her that Joe had left, leaving her to puzzle out how she'd gotten from resting against his broad shoulder in the living room to lying in her bedroom upstairs. Because, at five-eleven and at least ten pounds above her ideal weight, she wasn't exactly feather-light, so he couldn't have carried her.

Could he?

A vague, dream-like recollection of taking a very bumpy, rocking, laborious ride up the main staircase flashed through her mind, and Emma briefly contemplated calling all the area hospitals to see if they had a guy named Joe in traction. But then she was caught up by the thought of her head on Joe's broad shoulder last night, his arm around her body. Maybe he was strong enough to have hauled her up the steps without too much difficulty.

She walked through her house to the living room, which she'd decorated in sunny yellows with burnt-orange and gold accents to complement the sage couch where she and Joe had fallen asleep the night before. On top of the Asian apothecary-style coffee table sat a stack of paper, used on one side, and a pair of scissors—a project left over from when her life had been boring. Idly, she picked up some of the paper and started cutting it into quarters to use for scratch pads. Before long, she was cutting furiously, trying to keep her mind busy and off of what it felt like to fall asleep beside Joe Lopez.

Because let's say it again: she had no room for anyone in her life, he had…issues at the moment. Not to mention that whenever she spent time with him, she had a near-death experience. Analytically speaking, those should be enough reasons to send any sane person running as fast as they could in the opposite direction from Joe.

But noooo. Her mind agreed that putting him out of her head and getting him out of her life as fast as possible were two very good ideas, but her stupid body kept remembering that he had very nice shoulders. And nice arms, too. Arms that were perfectly capable of lifting one of the few women in L.A. who didn't resemble a size-two fish stick.

What if he'd gone?

It wasn't too far-fetched that Joe would decide that pursuing his past was simply becoming too dangerous for both of them. He very well could have gotten up in the middle of the night, leaving her and his traumatic past behind to go back to his office, his friends and that poor dog with the unfortunate name without so much as a "Dear Emma" note. She considered that thought for a moment.

She didn't like it.

Looking down at her busywork, Emma noticed that rather than cutting the paper into symmetrical quarters, she'd managed to create two small and two large trapezoids.

Nice.

Then the doorbell rang, and somehow, she knew it was Joe.

Which was just as well, because apparently she wouldn't be able to concentrate on anything until he came back anyway.

Answering the door confirmed that Joe had, indeed, returned. He'd obviously gone back to his hotel to shower and change into a clean pair of jeans and a gray Lakers T-shirt, probably his normal attire when not at the conference. Reaching up to finger comb her hair, she wished she hadn't slept so late so she could have done the same.

"Good morning," she said, then noticed

that Louis Bernard was standing beside Joe. "Well, hey, Louis."

"Hi," Louis replied, lifting one foot and balancing his weight fully on the other, kind of like a stork.

"You have a secret room in your house?" Joe asked.

Well, that was abrupt. "No, not that I know of."

"Mind if we come in?" he asked, his expression all business, with no hint that he'd been worrying over their night together as she had. Then again, a good-looking guy like Joe probably saw a lot more action than your average English prof stuck in a rut. Falling asleep on his shoulder had been the hottest night she'd had in ages.

Sad.

Blinking away her thoughts, Emma stepped back to let them pass. "Sure." Then, as Louis shuffled down the hall, his bare feet scuffing against the runner, she turned back to Joe, who was walking just fine despite having carried her upstairs the night before. "What's this all about, you and Louis?"

"Experiment," he said. "Hang on a sec."

Louis turned sharply into the living room, and Emma and Joe followed.

Gripping the lapels of his lime-green, short-sleeved shirt, Louis rocked back and forth on his heels in the middle of the room, humming the theme song to *Barney*.

"Okay, I'm dying to know what kind of experiment this is," said Emma, tossing her head as her voluminous hair fell into her eyes, "and if it has anything to do with your personal taste in music."

"Very funny," Joe retorted, standing elbow to shoulder with her and watching Louis with the intensity of a hawk. "Is it okay if I just let him look around the room for a minute?"

"Sure, but what—?"

"Met your neighbor." He propped himself against the doorjamb, watching Louis and waiting for…something.

Louis was busying himself with some small, brown-glazed Red Wing pottery bowls that were resting on top of the fireplace mantle.

"Louis?" She knew he'd answered her unfinished question with his pithy "met your neighbor" statement, but she was still confused. "You met him when you first came here."

"No, his mother."

"Oh, Jasmine? She's been in this neighborhood for…" Emma trailed off as understanding dawned, fighting the urge to smack herself in the forehead. "Wow, am I an idiot. She knew your family, didn't she?"

The corners of Joe's mouth tipped upward, and he nodded, but he kept his concentration on Louis, who had moved to the coffee table and was pulling out all the little apothecary drawers and then pushing them back. Emma quickly stepped forward to move the scissors out of harm's way, then returned to Joe's side.

"She knew me, too," he said. "Apparently, I had a thing for her Key lime pie when I was a kid. And since she happened to have some on hand, can't say that I blame myself."

Emma smiled. Leave it to Jasmine to conjure up a warm and happy image for Joe before the two strolled down Horrific Memory Lane.

"So." Emma crossed her arms. "What's all this about a secret room?"

Gesturing with his chin at Louis, who was now crouched in front of the fireplace and trying to look up the chimney, Joe got that faraway look in his eyes that he sometimes did when discussing his fragmented past. Fortunately, it wasn't the one where he did his Joe of the Living Dead act to accompany it. "He found me, the day after my mother was murdered. Jasmine thinks it was inside some secret compartment or room off of the living room." He hitched a shoulder in a singular shrug. "Makes sense that she hid me somewhere, or I'd probably be dead, too."

Emma shook her head, feeling a pang of regret at having to burst his lead. "I've been all over this house, sanding, scraping, applying nontoxic paint. If there was a secret room, I'd have found it, trust me. Maybe we should ask your friend, Detective Rodriguez, to take a look into the police records and see what they have to say about when and where you turned up after the murder."

For the first time since Louis began

scouring the room, Joe turned and looked at her, his otherworldly eyes sending a shiver down her spine. "What's up with all this environmental stuff?" he asked, giving her his half smile.

"What do you mean?"

"The Prius, the scratch paper on the table there, the nontoxic paint, that ugly bag of yours that has to be made out of recycled something—what are you, some kind of hippie?"

Not entirely surprised that Joe had been that observant, Emma straightened to her full height, taking a split-second to regret the fact that Joe was too tall for her to tower menacingly over. "It's a designer hemp satchel, FYI, and if caring about the environment and not wanting to die in a cloud of climate-changing noxious gas generated by all of our waste and pollution makes me a hippie, then I proudly wear that moniker. And furthermore…"

"Whoa, there, Jane Goodall." Laughing now, Joe held his hands out in front of him in mock surrender. "I just felt like spinning you up. It's cool."

Emma glared at him, then turned away to watch Louis smooth his hands across the fireplace bricks. "Just because you choose to drive a global-warming nightmare of a car—"

"I have compact fluorescents in my office," he interjected, obviously hoping it would win him some points.

Flicking a glance at his sneaker-clad feet, she crossed her arms and kept her scowl intact. "Your shoes were made in a sweatshop. Probably by small starving children."

"I'll send them back to the company. Look, Emma, I was kidding."

"And if your T-shirt were made of organic cotton, which it's not, it would have kept pounds of pesticides out of the atmosphere."

"Emma, if I'd known you were this sensitive…"

"I am not sensitive!"

"…I wouldn't have made that lame joke. I apologize. Deeply, humbly, and all that."

She paused, her mouth quirking a little at the corners. "Thank you. And you do know that some of that hysteria was feigned just to get back at you, right?"

He elbowed her gently. "I know."

She elbowed him back. "Good."

They stood together, still watching Louis when Joe broke the silence. "Hey, about that designer hemp satchel."

Emma put her hands over her ears. "Don't say it, please don't say it, please, please, please…"

"Could we smoke it?"

She was about to launch into her standard diatribe about how you'd have to smoke an industrial hemp joint the size of a tree to feel any effects, when… "Omigod."

"Kidding, Em. I don't do—" She sensed Joe look up mid-sentence and heard his sharp intake of breath as he saw what she had.

Louis had just managed to trip something in his explorations around the fireplace, because just to the right of it, in the corner of the room, a small panel had slid neatly to the side, revealing a dark, recessed hole in the wall. Just big enough for one small boy.

Chapter Eight

"I found it. I couldn't remember, because everything is in the wrong place, but then I remembered," Louis said, totally deadpan, his droopy dog expression unchanging.

Approaching Louis and the opening he'd revealed in the wall, Joe clapped his hand reassuringly on Louis's thin bicep. "Lou, buddy, you're the man."

"I'm the man," Louis parroted, appearing marginally happier at the compliment.

"You're *so* the man," Joe said, smacking Louis's arm lightly once more.

"I'm the man!" Smiling at last, Louis suddenly looked like he was about to jump in the air and click his heels together. Joe grinned back. Louis might be in his fifties, but there was something kind of cute about how his reserved, gentlemanly air contrasted with his bursts of childlike enthusiasm.

Caught up in looking at the hole, Joe didn't hear Emma come up behind him until they were shoulder to shoulder. She laid her hand gently on Joe's arm, echoing what he'd done with Louis moments before, and searched his face with her huge green eyes. For what, he wasn't sure, but he'd bet it had something to do with her expecting him to freak out.

"I'm fine," he said. Fact was, he'd been so excited about being right about the crawl space's existence that he hadn't even thought about what was going to happen, what he would remember, once he looked inside.

Just then, Emma grabbed his hand. She had twisted her thick curls into a loose braid, which managed to stay in place despite the fact that she had no rubber band to tie off the end. Focusing her green eyes on him, she squeezed his fingers. "I'm here, Joe," she said in her smoky, torch-song voice. "Let's take a look."

Pretty, thoughtful Emma. What he wouldn't give for them to have met under normal circumstances, so he could have tried his damnedest to make her fall for him. Because getting her shot at and scared to pieces in her own home probably hadn't won him any points so far. Not to mention the whole forgetting his childhood and acting like a general wing nut.

For now, he just let himself enjoy the feel of her slender hand inside his larger one. She may not have been petite, but everything about her, from her pretty hands to her long, loose curls to those incredible legs, made him think of the screen goddesses of the Thirties and Forties. And that was definitely a good thing.

He nodded and stepped forward, until the opening, which was approximately two feet by three feet, was directly before them.

"This wallpaper," Emma began, tracing the intricate tan-on-cream pattern with her fingers, "is original from the time the house was built. Or so said my Realtor. It was so well-preserved, I couldn't bear to replace it." She turned to him and shrugged. "Okay, I didn't sand and paint every surface. Sorry. But I did do most of them."

Crouching down, Joe examined the edges where the panel had been. "The wallpaper pattern made this door practically invisible."

"It sure did." She crouched beside him and peered inside.

Pulling his keys out of the pocket of his jeans, Joe flicked on the tiny flashlight attached to his keyring. The bulb wasn't any bigger than your average marble, but its light was deceptively bright. He stepped inside.

Interesting. "I can almost stand in here," he called to Emma.

"Seriously?" She stuck her head through the opening.

Shining the flashlight across the brick floor, Joe crouched down when he spotted a footprint. "Check this out," he said.

Emma leaned in farther to look where he was pointing. "Looks like a kid's tennis shoe."

"It's mine," he said. "See that whale pattern in the imprint? My shoes were designed to look like Nikes, but they had these long, thin blue whales on the side where the swoosh would have been. I liked them. Thought they were nonconformist."

Emma cocked her head at him. He scrubbed a hand over his eyes, which felt gritty from being in an enclosed space that hadn't received an infusion of fresh air in years. "Now there's a helpful detail," he said, laying the sarcasm on as thick as the dust in the air. "Glad I remembered that."

Emma shook her head. "Joe, it's something. The more that comes back to you, the better, even if they're just small things right now."

Not knowing how to respond to that, he kept searching the room. Three of the walls were brick, like the floor, and the fourth wall, the one adjoining the living room, was made of wood and plaster. Near that wall, he could see his boyish footprints one on top of the other, as if he'd been scrambling sideways in front of that wall.

Let me out…

Maybe he had been. Turning away from the footprints and their goddamned whales, Joe ran the beam along the room's corners.

Loose brick.

Moving swiftly to the far right corner, he bent down to peer at one of the floor bricks, which was slightly higher than the others around it and didn't have any cement around its edges. Slipping his fingers into one of the open edges, he pulled at the brick until it came up in a small cloud of dust. Its neighboring brick wobbled, and Joe pulled that one up, too.

Underneath was a small metal box. Carefully picking it up, Joe dusted it off and turned to carry it back into the living room. Something told him he'd found exactly what he was looking for.

He turned back to the opening. "I saw my father hiding this here once," he said. He moved to the couch, placing the box on the coffee table and sitting down. Emma sat next to him.

"Where's Louis?" he asked as he worked the catch with his fingers.

"He went home. Didn't like my current selection of Pop-Tarts," she responded, leaning in to watch him work. "Speaking of Louis, remember what he said about playing with you and Daniel in the tower? This room is right underneath the turret, which I thought was only open on the upstairs levels."

"Makes sense now," he said, still working on the box. When it was clear that it wouldn't open, he took a jackknife out of his pocket and pulled out the slimmest blade. A few seconds of artful jabbing with it, and the box opened.

"You do have a way with locks," Emma murmured, peering over his shoulder at the box.

Inside were copies of three letters, in a confident, spidery hand; a floppy disk that looked as if it had come out of an ancient Apple IIc or similar computer circa the late 1970s; and several canisters of camera film. Picking up the top letter from the small stack, Joe skimmed the contents.

"I don't have my glasses," Emma said behind him. "What does it say?"

He read the letter two or three times in silence, his gut twisting at the words. Then, after skimming the other two, he slowly set them down on the coffee table and read the first one aloud.

Dear Wade,
Enclosed you'll find several photos of you and your lady friend in, shall we say, compromising positions. Please call to discuss how we can keep this information out of the newspapers.
—Your Friend

"What does that mean?" Emma asked, reaching for the pieces of yellowed paper. She held the one he'd just read at arm's length and squinted at it. "It sounds almost like—"

"Blackmail," Joe finished, spitting out the ugly word. "The other letter has instructions on where to send payments, if I'm not mistaken. And the third piece of paper lists dates, times and locations, though I'm not sure of what. Probably something to do with the reason for the blackmail."

Emma flipped through the pages, then set them back down again. "Who's blackmailing who? Who's Wade?"

"That's the million-dollar question. Although my gut is telling me that is my father's handwriting." Reaching over to take a small glass globe from its stand on one of the end tables, Joe toyed with the blue sphere.

Emma sat silently beside him, obviously not knowing what to say about what they'd just learned about his proud family history.

Fighting the sudden urge to smash the globe against the nearest wall, Joe settled for clenching his fist around it. He put it back into its holder, a little harshly from the rattle it made, and pushed off the couch to pace the room.

He could remember them. For the first time in his life, he could see his father's face as well as his mother's, and he knew who they were with a dead, cold certainty. Pausing in front of an antique wood-framed mirror hanging on the wall, Joe studied his own features. He had his father's prominent nose and square jaw, his mother's light-brown eyes and thick, black hair. When he smiled, he knew it would be a combination of both of them.

Blackmailers. Instead of the parents he'd at last gotten to know in the past few days through the *Times* articles Emma had collected—brave people who'd served and protected the citizens of Los Angeles—they'd been two-bit blackmailers, and their greed had ruined not just their lives, but the lives of four others who hadn't deserved it.

He'd spent his entire life in foster care, with no recollection of his brothers and his sister. God only knew what conditions the twins had found themselves in. Had anyone wanted two five-year-old boys? Or had they just stayed in the system as he had, maybe without a Beth Billings to make them feel they'd belonged somewhere, had a home somewhere?

At least he could hope Sabrina was having a good life. Most people wanted to adopt little babies, didn't they?

"Joe, you're going to wear a hole in the rug."

Emma's words pulled him out of his thoughts, and the sight of her face made some of the tension leave his neck and shoulders.

"I think I might be able to fill in one of these missing pieces," she said. "Wait here."

She ran across the hall to the library, then returned a few seconds later with a manila folder in her hand. Rifling quickly through it, she selected one of the papers from the stack inside and handed it to Joe.

It was a copy of one of the newspaper clippings she'd collected about his parents. This one had a picture of his mother, standing next to a man whom the caption identified as Mayor Allen of Los Angeles. That man was now a California senator.

Ramon and Daniela may have been flawed, severely flawed, but they were still his parents. And the man in the fuzzy black-and-white photo he was holding, Senator *Wade* Allen, had had a motive to kill them.

"Dear Wade," he said softly.

"Exactly," she replied.

Chapter Nine

After extending his stay at the hotel under an alias, Joe spent the next week lying low and multitasking like a madman. He'd express mailed the ancient floppy disk to his assistant Teresa in San Francisco to work on retrieving the data and had sent the film they'd found to a photo studio in Arkansas, where the developers weren't likely to recognize a California senator if he appeared in the pictures. And he'd checked on Emma by phone every so often—fortunately, she'd received no more unwanted visitors, though unbeknownst to her, he either watched her house at night himself or had hired another investigator to do it for him on the nights when he needed sleep.

And, when he'd had a spare moment, he'd used it to visit just about every adoption agency in the greater Los Angeles area. Most were dead ends, but after hoofing it around the city all day, one woman at the Russell Agency—the second-to-last one on his list—had confirmed that they had facilitated the adoption of twin boys by a local family twenty-some years ago.

As soon as she'd asked him for the twins' specific birthdate, he had suddenly and without thinking spit out Nov. 2, 1973—the only memory of his past to surface since they'd found the secret room in Emma's house. He could tell by the woman's expression that the date he'd given her and the one in her computer had matched, but since it had been a closed adoption, she wouldn't give him any more information than she already had, citing confidentiality laws and the fact that she could get into serious trouble for giving him that much. So while he had a strong feeling he was sniffing up the right tree, he still didn't know for sure how old the boys listed in the agency's computer were, what their names had been, and, most important of all, what family had adopted them. But that was okay, because he did know the family had been living in Los Angeles, and he knew the twins' birthdate. Couple that with the probably safe assumption that they hadn't changed their first names, and Joe was golden. He'd found missing people before with less information than this.

The reality that his brothers were *close* hit him as he finally stopped to take a breath after the whirlwind of work he'd been caught up in all day. He had to admit, just the thought of them made him feel better about his parents, the blackmail, everything. He'd bring Daniela's and Ramon's killer to justice for his brothers, and then he'd tell them how sorry he was that he hadn't tracked them down years ago, when he'd been fresh out of UC Berkeley's criminal justice program, paid for by the Army G.I. bill, and just about to apply for his P.I. license. And then, together, they would find Sabrina. He wasn't naive enough to think that they'd all be one big happy family after that, but at least they wouldn't be just empty holes in his life, waiting to be filled.

Pushing aside thoughts of his parents' illegal activities, he picked up the tan plastic hotel phone on the cheap nightstand and dialed the work number of one of his friends. Lucas Franzetti was a San Francisco police detective and all-around good ·guy who, like all cops, had access to the national DMV database. More importantly, he had, in the past, demonstrated the willingness to do bizarre and only slightly illegal searches on said database, if Joe could come up with a very compelling reason·for him to do so. Fortunately, Joe was good at coming up with compelling reasons.

"Yo, Franzetti here." The detective's loud, nasal accent came through the phone loud and clear.

"Hey, Franzetti," Joe responded, "how 'bout those Lakers?"

He could practically hear Franzetti scowling at the phone. "Shut up, Lopez, you cocky SOB."

Joe laughed. "You live in California. You

should know better than to root for an out-of-state team, dude."

"Hey, you can take the boy out of Boston… The Celtics are my team, you know?"

"Yeah, whatever." Picking up a pencil that had been lying next to the phone, Joe flipped it around through his fingers. "That's fifty bucks and a case of beer you owe me when I get back, Franz, and I want the good stuff. Not that crap you're always drinking."

"That hurts, Joe. That really hurts." The good humor in Franzetti's voice belied his words.

"Hey," Joe said, taking a sudden turn for the serious. "You mind doing me a favor?"

He heard Franzetti sigh good-naturedly. "Oh, sure, what kind of illegal, immoral, my-bosses-would-put-my-butt-in-a-sling-if-they-found-out favor can I do for you now, Lopez?"

Rather than reminding Franzetti how many times he'd grilled his contacts and shared information to help the SFPD close a case, Joe just went for it. "I need you to do a DMV search in the state of

California for two brothers, born November 2, 1973, first names Patricio and Daniel."

"Twins?"

Joe could hear Franzetti's pencil scratching away. "Yeah."

"Last name?"

"Not sure. It was Lopez before they were adopted."

The silence that followed stretched on for several seconds, and all he could hear was a faint humming through the phone line. Finally, Franzetti found his voice again. "Joe, who are these guys? You said you didn't have any family, so is the last name just a coincidence?" Franzetti would know. Joe had spent most Thanksgivings and several Christmases with Lucas and his wife Gloria, a criminal defense lawyer who loved to cook, bless her and her miraculous cranberry-bread crumb stuffing.

"No. They're my brothers."

Letting out a long, low whistle, Franzetti paused once more, presumably to let that information sink in. "Okay, Lopez the elder," he said, "I have a couple of things to attend to, but I'll do your search later this afternoon. Call you after five?"

"That's great, man," Joe responded, relief zinging through his veins. Not that he hadn't thought Franz would come through for him, but there was always that slim chance… "I owe you."

"What you owe me is the background on this little family reunion of yours. I had no idea," Franzetti said. "Brothers. Huh."

When they'd hung up, Joe fired up his computer again and logged onto Metro-Files.net, one of the many information databases made available to private detectives through the magic of direct mail. Back in 2000, MetroFiles had taken that year's U.S. census data, merged it with listed telephone numbers, property records and other information sources in the public domain, and had come up with a handy searchable database, updated regularly, that would spit out all kinds of information on unsuspecting citizens across the country. It had taken months of trying out several junk databases from numerous sources to find the excellent MetroFiles. But now, for the bargain price of $50 a month, the perfectly legal system had proven its worth to Joe time and again in his missing persons work. And now that he had a birthdate to plug in, plus first names, maybe MetroFiles would work its magic once more. He also had access to three similar databases, but he always tried MetroFiles first.

Just as he finished plugging his scant information into the required fields, someone knocked softly on his door.

"Just a sec," he called, as he clicked his mouse on the Search button in the bottom right corner of the screen.

"It's me."

Emma. He'd recognize that screen-goddess voice even through a steel door.

Jumping up from the bed, Joe let her inside.

"How's your day been? Have you made any progress?" she asked, bounding across the room with large strides that caused her flowing pale green dress to swirl around her knees. With none of the painful propriety she'd displayed the last time she'd come to his hotel room, she sat down on the bed with enough energy that she nearly sprung back up again.

He narrowed his eyes at her, wondering what she was so darn happy about. "A little. Found enough information to do a database search for Patricio and Daniel." He gestured toward the laptop that lay on his bed, connected by a thin cable to the hotel phone. "And by the way, Em, how much sugar did you put in your Wheaties this morning?"

"It was organic kasha, thank you very much, and I have a surprise for you." Bracing herself with both hands on the mattress, she bounced slightly as she spoke.

"I hate surprises," he said, still standing at the foot of the bed.

"You'll like this one." Glancing over at his laptop, which was facing her, she reached over to tilt the screen so she could see it better. "It says, 'System down from 8:00 to 11:30 p.m. for maintenance.' Was this one of your searches?"

Striding forward, Joe spun the computer around so he could see it. He swore as soon as he saw the error message. "Great timing."

Emma winced at his expression. "I'm sorry. That's really frustrating. But maybe this will help." Reaching toward the floor, she picked up her hemp satchel with one hand and hefted it onto the blue-and-green quilted bedspread. "So you were probably asking yourself, 'Now that Senator Wade Allen is our chief suspect in the Lopez murders, how am I going to get close enough to him to start pelting him with incisive, probing questions?'"

"Uh, sure," Joe muttered, still peeved about the ill-timed MetroFiles maintenance. "That's exactly what I was asking myself. And what's up with this 'our suspect' business? You should probably leave the country."

"No chance," she said swiftly. "But as I was eating the aforementioned organic kasha this morning, I remembered reading about Senator Allen holding a benefit ball tonight for his major donors and other VIPs."

"And just how much does attending this ball cost?" He leaned back against the wall, next to the TV set and its cherry-stained wooden stand, expecting her to name an exorbitant amount.

She flipped a hand at him. "That's exactly what I wanted to know. So I called up Senator Allen's office and asked." Rolling up the sleeves of her blue crocheted cardigan sweater, she unfastened the top flap of her satchel and started fishing around inside. "See, I put some money aside every year to make political and charitable contributions to people and causes I think are going to make a difference. I tend to do it all at once at the end of the year, so I still had all five thousand dollars in my political account."

He didn't think he was going to like where she was going with this.

"Anyway," she said, pulling a wad of receipts and a zippered plastic bag filled with tissues out of her bag, "I've made some fairly good-sized contributions to Senator Allen during his reelection campaign last year. He has a very exciting plan for increasing solar energy use in the state of California, which could catalyze the growth of the solar industry across the U.S.

by making it more affordable." She placed a couple of energy bars next to the tissues.

"So, you were telling me about your five thousand dollars," Joe reminded her.

"Right. So anyway, I ask the aide how much two tickets would cost, and guess what he says?"

"Uh, five thousand dollars?"

"Yes! So I ran over there with a check, and voilà!" With a flourish, she pulled an envelope with her address showing through a clear plastic window and the AT&T logo out of the bag.

"They paid your phone bill?"

She glanced at the envelope in her hand and tossed it to the side, once more sticking her hand inside her satchel. "Whoops. Here we go. Voilà!" This time, her hand came out clutching a plain white envelope with Senator Wade Allen's address embossed in red in the upper left corner.

"That would be two tickets to tonight's ball, I take it?" he asked, folding his arms.

She nodded and handed him the envelope. He shook the tickets out of it, which showed that the ball started at 8 p.m. at the

Millennium Biltmore Hotel on Grand Avenue. Apparently, his plans for running database searches had just turned into an evening rubbing elbows with a bunch of cake-eaters.

"Nice work," he said, meaning it, at which Emma grinned at him, looking more girlish and less elegant than he'd ever seen her. Apparently, detective work suited her. Which was so not good, seeing as waving Emma under the nose of the man who may have been terrorizing her all week wasn't exactly what he thought of as a stellar idea.

"Look, I'll pay you back," he said, mentally calculating how much money he could scrape together if he emptied his nonretirement investment accounts and sold the 1950s Mustang GT he'd been restoring by hand for the past few years.

"Are you kidding me?" Crossing her legs, she leaned back on her palms. "Read my lips—that money was earmarked for political contributions. I just boosted Allen's solar plans or took you another step closer to bringing a killer to justice. Either way, it's money well spent, in my opinion."

"I'll pay you back," he said again.

She straightened abruptly, sitting on the bed like she had a metal rod inserted inside her spine. "You will not! There's no need. I like social events like this."

"Emma—"

"Joe." She raised an eyebrow, her voice pitched lower than usual. "Continue to argue with me, and I'll take Louis and leave you at home."

"Okay, okay, I give up. For now." He stepped forward and sat next to her on the bed. "But Emma, I don't think it's such a good idea that you go. If Allen is the one who killed my parents, he might just come after you if he sees us together. I mean, right now things are quiet because he thinks I left the city."

She sobered instantly. "I know. But you're not going to go to this thing by yourself, and I am your ticket in." She waved the envelope at him. "Literally."

"I work better alone," he said. It was true, actually.

"Joe, let me put it this way—you'd have to tie me to this bed to keep me from going with you." As soon as she'd finished the sentence, her face turned an interesting shade of crimson, and they both looked at the bed, then at each other. Joe's eyes dropped to her mouth, and his lips turned upward in a small, private smile.

"I need to go change, and you have exactly—" she checked her watch, her words coming out in rapid-fire succession "—three hours to find a tux. So, I'm going to go. Okay, then. Bye." And with that, she was out the door, leaving Joe chuckling behind her.

BACK AT HOME, clad only in a slip and a pair of black control-top pantyhose, Emma rifled through the dresses in one of the too-tiny Victorian bedroom closets. Really, she didn't know what she was rifling for. She only had two formals—one, a navy blue floor-length gown with spaghetti straps and a short-sleeved lace jacket; the other, a vintage silver gown from the 1930s that somehow managed to hug her curves while miraculously flattening her stomach. Pulling them out of her closet, she held them out in front of her. Which to choose—the blue, which made her look like an elderly first lady, or the silver, which was a little more daring than she usually felt comfortable in?

One thought of being on Joe's arm, and she knew she couldn't face him looking like a first lady.

Pulling the silver material over her head, she inserted her arms into the proper holes and smoothed the satin down her hips. The Thirties-style draped front was only a little revealing, but the back was cut all the way down to the small of her back, and she couldn't help but feel naked, despite the fact that everything that had to be covered was. Heading back into her bedroom, she took an opal pendant off her vanity and fastened it around her neck, adding the matching drop earrings. A few strategically placed pins in her hair, and she had an elegant upsweep, softened by a few curls she'd pulled loose to give herself a slightly Grecian look.

Just as she'd finished, the doorbell rang. Joe.

With one knee propped on her chaise lounge, Emma unlocked her bedroom window and raised it, sticking her head out. "Come on in, the door's open," she called once she'd confirmed it was indeed her date for the evening.

She heard him come inside and instantly a flurry of butterflies took off inside her stomach. It might have been a favor, but heaven help her, it felt like a real date.

Taking a deep breath, Emma slipped into her low-heeled shoes and walked to the top of the stairs.

As she'd expected, Joe stood at the bottom, looking way better in his tuxedo than any man had a right to look. His normally tousled hair had been combed back off his forehead, and the way the tux draped perfectly across his shoulders screamed Rodeo Drive.

Something had changed in the past week, she realized. She'd missed him, missed his presence since they'd only talked by phone. And by the expression on his face, it seemed he might have missed her as well.

Looking up the stairs at her, Joe exhaled, long and slow, his eyelids lowering slightly so his eyes looked hooded. "That's a dress," he said.

She couldn't help herself. Accepting compliments had never been easy for her. "Yes, Joe, it is a dress. A very big dress, for a very big woman."

"Hardly." After uttering that one word, which made her feel marginally less naked, he just watched her descend the staircase. And although it was a prom-night cliché played out in way too many teen films, she liked being watched. A little too much.

When she reached the bottom, feeling a little shaky after twenty-four steps taken under Joe's otherworldly gaze, Joe held out his arm, and she wrapped her hand around his elbow. Then he leaned toward her, so that his mouth was close to her ear. "You look beautiful," he whispered, and she could feel his breath on her skin.

She tried to say thank you, but it just came out as a warbly squeak. Something had definitely changed.

"And don't get me started on your body." He hadn't moved. Neither had she.

"Why not?" she asked, finally recovering her grasp of the English language. She turned slightly toward him, all too aware as the space between them grew smaller. Her eyes focused on his crisp, black shoulder.

"Because you'd either kiss me or hit me if I told you what I was thinking, and I'm not sure either is a good idea."

Emma swallowed. "Why don't you tell me anyway?"

He just looked at her for several seconds. She wasn't sure who leaned forward first, but soon his mouth was on hers, his lips warm as he kissed her with a gentleness that made her afraid she wouldn't be able to keep standing for much longer.

When they finally pulled apart, she was clinging to his shoulders, and his arm was around her waist, his other hand cupped around the nape of her neck. He trailed his fingers across her skin until they gently pulled one of the loose curls near her temple straight.

"You're beautiful," he said again. "You

took my breath away when you came down the stairs."

Emma reached forward and straightened his tie—a long, black length of silk, rather than the standard bow tie. "I could say the same. You clean up well, Mr. Lopez."

He smiled at her, a flash of white teeth against tan skin, and held his elbow out once more. "So do you, Dr. Reese. Can't say I'm missing the layers of clothes you usually mummify yourself in."

Just as she opened her mouth to shoot off some indignant reply, he leaned over and kissed her briefly. "Ready to go?"

What had she been about to say? "Okay," she replied lamely.

They left through the back door, as had been her habit since the visit from the sniper. Not that it would keep anyone from following them—their exit still would be easy for anyone who was watching to notice. But they were safely inside Emma's Prius—which she'd insisted on taking since it got better gas mileage than the car he'd traded in his original rental for—by the time they hit the street.

As Joe pulled the Prius out of the driveway, Emma noticed a dark brown sedan pulling away from the curb a few car lengths down the street.

"Joe, did you see that?"

"I saw it," he confirmed, scowling blackly into the rearview mirror. He drove the car leisurely down June Street, the sedan staying well behind them.

They cruised slowly past the Victorian homes and newer houses of Hancock Park. Rather than checking out the new paint jobs or landscaping efforts she usually loved to see, she kept quiet and watched the car behind them through the passenger side mirror. He was good, whoever he was. He kept at least one car in between them and hung back far enough that if they hadn't already been hyperaware of potential threats, they probably would have missed him entirely.

Suddenly, Joe gave the steering wheel a yank, and the car spun around, tires squealing. Clutching the door handle, Emma held on for all she was worth, until the Prius came to a halt, facing the direction from which they'd come. She found herself face to face with the man who'd been following them.

Rodriguez.

Surprise evident on his features, even though half of his face was covered by his mirrored glasses, Rodriguez kept driving forward, until he turned at the next block and disappeared. As if he'd been out for a leisurely drive that had just happened to take him into her neighborhood.

"I really need to have a talk with that guy," Joe muttered, and they rode to the ball in silence. Emma could only continue picturing Rodriguez as the one who had chased them through her neighborhood, who'd wrapped her scarf around her neck like he would choke her. A sociopath hidden behind a badge, protected by his brotherhood in blue. It wasn't a comforting thought.

She stared out the window, wondering when he would try again, and if they'd survive it next time.

Chapter Ten

As they walked into the Biltmore's Gold Room, Emma on Joe's arm, she couldn't help but feel as if she'd wandered into a palace. Magnificent Austrian crystal chandeliers hung above them, softly illuminating the thirty-foot ceiling, hand-painted in the style of the Spanish Renaissance. Floor-to-ceiling mirrors decorated the hardwood-paneled walls, and several small balconies dotted the far wall, dusty rose brocade curtains fanning above them and over the ballroom's many windows.

A long table with refreshments took up an entire side of the room, and the other was occupied by dancers and a twenty-one-piece big band. Circular tables covered with white linen cloths and artfully placed floral arrangements were scattered around the dance floor, and the room was filled with California VIPs in designer tuxedos and gowns, the women wearing outrageously expensive rented jewels. Emma fingered her opal pendant, appreciating its simple beauty even more as a woman with the gaudiest ruby and diamond chandelier earrings she'd ever seen passed by.

"Ouch," Joe commented.

"No kidding," Emma said. "I wouldn't be surprised if she were hunched over and dragging those things on the ground by the time the evening is over."

"Real?"

"Of course. This is L.A."

"I don't get it. That's gotta hurt." Then, the earrings-slash-torture devices forgotten, he inclined his head toward the bar and raised his eyebrows in a silent question. She nodded and together they made a circuit of the room, checking out every sixty-something man with a full head of steel-gray hair they saw to no avail. Apparently the senator hadn't yet arrived.

As they passed the group of guests in

formal wear clustered around the open bar, Joe deftly plucked two glasses of champagne from a passing waiter. "One glass," he said, handing one of the flutes to Emma. "Don't want to get smashed in the enemy's camp. I'll get us sodas once the mob at the bar moves on."

Since he hadn't yet arrived, Emma felt it was safe to assume that the senator would enter the ballroom to all sorts of fanfare, so she let herself relax for a moment. Apparently, Joe felt the same, as he seemed happy to stop their rounds. He'd finished his champagne, so he deposited her next to a potted plant to head for the bar to get them both nonalcoholic drinks. As the band struck up "Stars Fell on Alabama," Emma took a sip of her champagne, stepping back closer to the wall when another couple needed to get past her.

A large, hard body stopped her progress, and she barely missed slopping champagne all over herself as her body jerked forward at the contact. "Excuse me," she said, running her finger up the glass to catch the bit that had lapped over the edge as she craned her head to see who was behind her.

A very tall man in Armani looked down at her with cool blue eyes. "No problem," he muttered, having already returned his gaze to a point above her head.

Emma watched him disappear into the crowd. "Odd."

"No," Joe said as he came up beside her, holding two Cokes. "Security."

Putting her champagne down on the nearest table, Emma reached for a Coke. She'd never been able to hold her alcohol, and even that one glass might make her do something stupid. Like hang all over Joe and tell him how very fine he looked in that tux. "How do you know? He looked like your average Hollywood VIP to me. Attitude and everything."

"Trust me, I know. It's the way he scanned the room, the way he was skulking in a corner like that, the way he moves." He shrugged. "He's security. I'd bet my dog on it."

Just then, the band went into an arrangement of "Strangers in the Night," heavy on the strings.

"They're playing our song," Joe whispered in her ear. He'd folded his body in toward her, so his arm was around her waist and his head was tipped close to hers.

Emma laughed softly, eyes on the point where his hair brushed against his collar, all too aware of how close they were standing. "So 'our song' is what a potentially homicidal maniac was whistling when he attacked us. Your sense of romance is just blowing me away, Joe."

She looked up into his face and found, to her surprise, that he wasn't smiling. In fact, his expression was intense, and she could have sworn he was going to kiss her. She tipped her chin upward, just a little. He came closer.

"Wanna dance?" he whispered against her lips.

Not knowing whether to shake him or finish what he'd started, Emma took the third option: she backed away. "All right."

But soon, she was back in his arms, one hand on his broad shoulder, the other clasped inside his larger one. He'd lowered his head so his face was almost touching her cheek, and his hand was on the bare skin of her back, sending chills shooting across her body every time he moved his fingers. As he expertly guided her around the floor, she reached around his neck to brush the hair at his collar with her fingertips. She wasn't inexperienced, though she was choosy about the men she'd dated, but she had to admit, dancing with Joe was quite possibly the most erotic moment of her life. She leaned forward to lay her head on his shoulder.

"You don't slouch." Joe's murmur interrupted her thoughts.

"Wha—?" Emma lcancd back and shot him a bewildered look. "Okay, you don't smell. Two can play at the random personal comment game."

He flashed his perfect smile at her, and it struck her how rarely he did that. Most of the time, he was being Mr. Very Serious and Important P.I. of the Year, or he just looked haunted, which usually meant a piece of his memory was slipping back into place.

"Nah," he said. "It's not as random as

you think. You had to shrink down to put your head on my shoulder, and it made me think about how rarely you do that. Shrink, I mean. I've known a lot of tall women who've seemed embarrassed by being tall. You don't. Just an observation."

Emma thought about that for a moment. "You know, when I was younger, getting dates was never easy for me. First, I resembled a praying mantis as a teenager, which kept the guys away. Then, once I grew into my long legs and arms, I was taller than most of the guys I was interested in. And then, once I started college, I was too bookish, which kept the guys away."

"What keeps them away now? That can of Mace in your purse?" The music stopped briefly, and then the band struck up another slow number—"Skylark"—into which Joe segued beautifully.

"Ha, ha. Very funny."

"Seriously, I know a lot of tall women who seem to wish they were four inches shorter, and it shows when they walk. And you have more confidence in your little finger than they do in their whole bodies."

"Is that a bad thing?" she asked, wondering if she needed to rip into a lecture on feminism in the twenty-first century.

"It's sexy as hell."

That grin of his was back, and she ducked her head to avoid letting Joe see that she was about to go up in flames. After taking a few seconds to compose herself, Emma did her best to convey cool amusement. "I'm tall. I'm not going to apologize for it."

"You don't have to."

The song ended, and then the band broke into a fanfare that had everyone backing off the dance floor and looking at the door. A couple of serious-looking men that Emma had no trouble pinpointing as security swept through the door and backed into the crowd, and then Senator Allen and his wife, Amelia Rosemont Allen, entered the room to the sounds of applause.

The senator made his way around the circle of people, Mrs. Allen trailing behind him, shaking hands and exchanging greetings with just about everyone on the outer rim. Emma hung back behind a woman with a blue bugle-beaded dress and what appeared to be two dates, not sure how wise it was for them to draw the senator's attention. As the senator approached their side of the room, Emma saw Joe move past her out of the corner of her eye. Before she could react, he was on the outside edge of the circle, and the senator was just three persons away from him.

When Emma noticed the murderous scowl on Joe's face, she threaded through the swarm of people and stumbled to Joe's side, tripping over someone's sweep train. "Relax, Joe," she whispered in his ear. "We're not going to get anything out of Senator Allen if you insist on looking like a sociopath. Or, at the very least, a member of the other party."

His shoulders rose as he inhaled deeply, then schooled his features into a more socially acceptable expression of polite interest. His golden eyes still had a dangerous look about them, but Emma hoped no one else would be looking at him that closely.

Senator Allen moved toward them, grasping the hand of the woman with the bugle beads and cupping her elbow with his other hand.

Joe straightened, his prior life in the military evident in his ramrod posture.

Emma quelled her urge to cower behind him. After all, she knew the Whistling Man and the senator were not the same person—the senator was shorter than their attacker had been, and she doubted he could have disguised his melodious Southern accent very well, a leftover from a childhood spent in Virginia. He'd had a cameo in a comedy film not too long ago, and wooden didn't even begin to describe the man's acting.

The senator let go of the woman's hand and turned his body toward Emma and Joe, but then the woman called him back for one more exchange. Emma clutched Joe's elbow, barely able to contain her impatience.

The senator turned.

Joe held out his hand.

Senator Allen slid his palm against Joe's.

And then he looked up into Joe's face. His hand jerked as if he were going to pull it back out of Joe's grasp, and the color left his soft, slightly wrinkled cheeks. But almost immediately, Allen recovered, and he shook Joe's hand with a firm, assured grip.

"Why, excuse me, son. Had a moment of déjà vu," Allen said heartily, nearly knocking them over with the force of his famous charisma. The senator was far from wooden in person, bad acting ability aside. "You look like someone I knew once, a long time ago."

"This is my date, Emma Jensen Reese." Joe gestured toward Emma. "And I'm Joe Lopez, Senator. My parents called me José Javier." Emma thought that it would have been hard for the senator to miss the challenge in Joe's eyes.

However, he showed no signs of recognition or fear this time, having recovered nicely from his earlier surprise. "Nice to meet you." He turned away from Joe to focus his attention on Emma. "And Dr. Jensen Reese. What a pleasure to see you again."

Emma wasn't surprised that the senator had recognized her. His gift for remembering names and faces was legendary throughout the state and in Washington.

She'd just about finished thanking him when Joe moved back into Allen's line of vision.

"My parents were LAPD, Senator. Daniela and Ramon Lopez. They were murdered back in 1978, when you were mayor." Joe coolly delivered the statement, but the threat in the air was almost palpable.

Just then, Amelia Allen caught up with her husband, moving to stand at his side. "Wade, why don't you tell me who these nice people are?"

Emma had actually had fairly long conversations with Mrs. Allen on several occasions, but Amelia apparently didn't share her husband's gift for names—she'd never shown the slightest hint of recognition when she'd seen Emma, and this time was no different. Her eyes looked slightly glazed as she patted her pale blond upsweep and gave them a vague smile.

"I remember your parents," Senator Allen said, his expression somber but betraying nothing. "You're the spitting image of your father."

Joe nodded curtly, a muscle in his jaw moving as he clenched his teeth.

Senator Allen put an arm around his wife and patted her back gently. "This is Joe Lopez and Emma Jensen Reese, dear. Dr. Jensen Reese is a regular donor to our campaign."

Amelia held out a limp hand, and Emma wasn't sure if she wanted her to shake it or kiss it. Emma opted for the former.

"Much obliged, Dr. Jensen Reese. We are so grateful for all donations to Wade's campaign. It all helps us make California better." Her last words echoed the senator's campaign slogan.

Beside her, Emma could feel Joe's body thrumming with pent-up energy. His scowl was creeping back into his face, and she knew it was just a matter of time before something very bad went down. So she moved in front of him and shook the senator's hand one more time. Amelia had already moved on. "Thank you, Senator. I really hope your solar plan takes off soon. I admire what you're trying to do. It was great seeing you. Bye!"

And then, like the babbling fool she was, she smiled brightly and backed into Joe, pushing him back into the crowd of people, who were only too happy to push forward and take their places in line.

As soon as she had him in front of a gilded wall, Emma turned on Joe. "What was that? The man might be trying to kill you, and you're challenging him like some maniacal professional wrestler?"

Joe was still scowling, and he apparently hadn't heard a word she'd said. She smacked him lightly on the shoulder. "Joe?"

He blinked and the scowl softened a bit. "Sorry, Emma. I had to do it." Then his eyes returned to the senator, who was finishing up his rounds with Amelia. "He recognized me."

Though still somewhat skeptical about the intelligence of Joe's MO, she agreed that the senator had seemed startled by Joe. "I think he did."

With that, Joe moved past her, as if he were planning on making a lunge for Wade Allen. Emma reached out and grabbed his elbow.

"Just what do you think you're doing?"

He stopped, glancing down at her hand around his arm. "Just going to shadow our friend the senator for awhile. See if he stops to have a suspicious conversation or takes out his cell phone and says, 'Hey, the guy whose parents I killed is here.'"

"I can't believe you can joke about this," she said.

A look of what could have been fear crossed his face, but it was gone as quickly as it had come. "Emma, I have to joke. Because otherwise, I'd kill him."

Feeling suddenly chilled, Emma dropped her hand.

"Don't worry. He won't even see me." With that, Joe melted into the glittering crowd, and try as she might, Emma couldn't spot him again. The guy was good, she'd give him that.

After a few futile minutes of scanning the masses for Joe, she spun around, intending to grab another soda at the bar. The movement brought her face to upsweep with Amelia Rosemont Allen.

"Ah, Dr. Johansen Cleese." The woman

trailed her beautifully manicured fingers up and down the thin stem of her wine glass. "Thank you again for your contributions to my husband's campaign."

"You're very welcome," Emma replied, deadpan. "All of us in the Johansen Cleese family are so pleased to support the senator."

"Oh, your whole family? How wonderful."

Emma could see Amelia mentally tallying the donation figures from all of the various and sundry Johansen Cleese relatives. Figuring she had the woman's ear now, Emma couldn't help but ask the question that had been uppermost in her mind since she'd made her very first donation to the Allen campaign. "I greatly admire the senator's work on solar energy, but I'm wondering whether he's going to follow through with his promise to push for greater tax incentives for alternative vehicles. The demand for hybrids is so high now, I wish that people had more of a financial reason to opt for them rather than a gas-guzzler."

Amelia Allen put a hand on her collarbone and gasped. "I was telling him the same thing just the other day. My daughter just bought a gas-electric hybrid car, and the price on it was much higher than a comparable conventional car. It's highway robbery, I tell you."

Emma laughed. "I really think more people would be buying them if consumers thought they were getting a bargain on the purchase price as well as when they pay for gas."

Amelia reached out and patted Emma's arm. "I'll have Wade send you a letter detailing his plans on that, I promise. I'm sure he has your address on file. He remembers everyone."

To her surprise, Emma believed her. "I'd appreciate that."

"Of course." Just then, something caught Amelia's eye over Emma's shoulder, and she clucked her tongue. "Oh, there's your beau."

Emma turned to see Joe watching them from across the room. He raised two fingers to his temple and then disappeared into the crowd once more.

"Ah, how he looks at you. With such light in his eyes." Amelia smiled softly and patted her arm once more. "You're a very lucky girl. Wade still looks at me like that, and it makes me just giddy every time."

It was such a sweet and genuine statement, coming from the normally polished and reserved Amelia, that Emma couldn't help but rethink her former opinions about the woman being a little cold. After all, constantly being in the public eye would make anyone think twice about everything that came out of one's mouth. "Sounds like you're lucky, too."

Amelia sighed, and both of them looked at her husband, still working the room. "Oh, yes. Public life has its challenges, but Wade makes it all worth it." She turned and winked at Emma. "But if that man of yours even hints about running for mayor, I strongly suggest that you nip it in the bud by suggesting a fulfilling alternative career." With that, Amelia patted her one more time and made her way toward her husband.

A few seconds later, Joe materialized at her side. "The senator is about to make a speech. Wanna bail?"

Emma stifled the urge to jump as the sound of his voice startled her. "I thought you were lying in wait for him to slip up and reveal all."

Joe put his hand on the small of her back, his thumb brushing the area where skin met dress. His touch was driving her crazy, in a good way. "Actually, I wanted to watch him, see if anything jolted loose in my head."

"Did it?"

"No." Joe's expression hardened, and Emma could feel the tension coming off him in waves. She put her hand on his back and steered him toward the door.

Together, they walked out of the ballroom and took the elevator to the magnificent lobby, a grand room lined with gilded columns and potted palms in marble containers, with an even more ornate handpainted ceiling than the Gold Room's. With not a little regret at leaving such beauty behind, Emma followed Joe out the door to the building's adjacent multilevel parking garage. A few minutes and a short walk later, they exited the garage elevator and headed to the far side of the fourth floor, where Emma's car waited. They walked in companionable silence, the only sounds being Emma's heels echoing on the concrete and the muffled noise of engines on floors above and below them.

Plucking the keys out of her beaded clutch, Emma turned to Joe. "I'll drive," she said, figuring he didn't need to be operating heavy machinery while so preoccupied. Joe nodded in agreement and headed for the passenger side of the Prius when they'd finally reached it.

Somewhere nearby, Emma heard a car door slam. The sound was ridiculously comforting, letting her know they weren't alone on their floor. But that cmfort was short-lived as a small slip of paper tucked under her windshield wiper caught her eye.

Feeling an immediate adrenaline rush at the thought of being busted by L.A.'s finest, Emma automatically checked the floor to make sure they'd parked in a bona fide spot and not a fire lane. They had.

"Ticket or flyer?" Joe asked.

"Flyer, I think," she replied, reaching

out to pull the white sheet of paper out from under the windshield wiper. It was blank on one side, so she flipped it over.

LEAVE.

The word was printed in large, block letters, almost perfectly formed, as if they'd been stenciled. A warm breeze blew through the open sides of the building and across her face, lifting the loose pieces of Emma's hair. Warm or not, it did little to combat the chill that had suddenly enveloped her body.

She looked up at Joe and flipped the paper around so he could see what it said.

Joe spun around, checking out all corners of the garage, his hand inside his jacket, where Emma knew his gun was holstered.

A shadow moved in the doorway to the fire exit on the opposite wall.

Before Emma could even open her mouth to tell him what she'd seen, Joe had taken off, his body a blur as he ran toward the far corner of the building.

Chapter Eleven

Ahead of him, Joe could see a shadow standing in the doorway to the stairwell, mocking him with its nearness. As soon as Joe was close enough that the shadow coalesced into the shape of a man, it turned and started running down the stairs. No casual observer, this.

Bursting through the steel fire door, Joe followed, pushing himself so he descended faster than the footsteps in front of him. He could see the man's hand on the metal banister, using it for leverage as he spiraled down toward the street.

Joe would be damned if he got there first.

Moving so fast that his feet barely touched the ground as he circled down, Joe took the steps two or three at a time. His burst of speed closed the gap between them until he caught a glimpse of the man's back as he rounded the next corner. Finally, when they were approaching the ground floor and there was only one set of stairs separating them, Joe grasped the banister and swung his body over it.

Landing ten feet below where he'd jumped jarred him to his very bones, but he remained standing, feet planted firmly apart. Unable to completely stop his momentum, the man he'd been chasing skidded down the rest of the stairs, coming to a stop just in front of Joe.

It was the security guard Emma had bumped into, back at the ball.

"I knew I didn't like you when I saw you," Joe growled.

The man smiled, though his ice blue eyes were colder than any Joe had ever seen. He moved suddenly to the left. Joe matched his movement.

He feinted right and moved left again. Again Joe matched him.

The man swung. Joe deflected the blow and landed a punch on the man's chiseled jaw with an audible slap of skin on skin. The man staggered backward.

"Where's your pretty date?" he asked Joe, swiping at a trickle of blood at the corner of his mouth. "Pretty, pretty Emma."

"Who are you working for?" His hands held protectively in front of him, Joe simply waited, refusing to rise to the man's bait.

"Who says I'm working for anyone?" Looking at Joe from beneath hooded eyelids, the man seemed unhurried, calm.

"I think you're too stupid not to be taking orders."

As soon as Joe had finished, the man lunged again. Joe caught him by the throat and used the man's own momentum against him, half pushing, half throwing him against the opposite wall. Before the man had a chance to recover, Joe had pushed his own forearm against the man's throat, his other hand pulling his gun out of his side holster and holding it against the man's temple.

"Who are you?" Joe snarled.

The man didn't answer. He clutched Joe's forearm, his chin raised to get as much air into his lungs as possible. But he remained outwardly calm. "Your father begged me not to kill him," he gasped.

Barely able to contain his sudden fury, Joe shoved his forearm hard against the man's throat. "Shut up."

The man's smarmy smile was back. "Your mother screamed when she died." He stopped, raised his chin higher and took a shuddering breath. "I would have finished you, too. Hidden away behind that panel, crying to be let out, but my employer had a soft spot for kids."

"Shut up!" His gun hand was trembling now, his trigger finger itching to press down. Behind him, through the red haze of his rage, he barely registered the sound of fast footsteps scuffling along the stairs above them.

The ice blue eyes were almost twinkling. "Her face was destroyed after I shot her. They had to identify her with dental records. Meanwhile, her little loser son cowered in the corner."

With an almost primal shout, Joe slammed his gun against the wall next to the man's head. Taking advantage of the moment, the man pushed Joe's forearm away and jerked his head forward so it slammed against Joe's skull.

The world blurred, and Joe stumbled backward as the stairwell tipped sideways, then righted itself again. Before he could recover, the man moved suddenly, and a pain sharper than any he'd ever known burst through his head. He clutched at his forehead, dropping his gun. His hand connected with a sticky wetness.

"Who's stupid now, Lopez?" the man asked, coughing in between his words. "You should have killed me. Hope you like your present." The man pushed past him, no doubt heading for the exit.

Joe collapsed against the stairwell, his vision clouding until he was unable to see anything but blurry light and dark surfaces. As his hands scrabbled against the rough concrete surface of the wall, he heard the footsteps come closer and the sound of an aerosol can being sprayed.

And then he saw nothing but darkness.

"JOE? OH, GOD, JOE, please wake up. Dammit, where's my cell phone? Joe, wake up." As close to hysteria as she'd ever been in her life, Emma dumped the contents of her clutch purse onto the ground next to Joe's inert body, remembering as soon as her lipstick, tissues and keys hit the floor that the bag's small size had forced her to choose between her phone and a can of pepper spray. She'd chosen the latter, and now, if that horrible man walked anywhere near a UV light in the next few days, he'd fluoresce like a cheap diner sign.

Grabbing the tissues off the ground, she discarded the one that had been in contact with the sticky floor, then cupped Joe's chin in one hand and blotted the blood running down his face with the other. Every so often, she'd stop to jostle his shoulder. "Joe, come on, wake up." Without a phone, she either had to leave him here and run for help, or somehow get him up the stairs to her car. Leaving him was no option.

She jostled him again, and this time, he stirred. "Let me out," he murmured.

"You're not trapped anymore, Joe. It's

Emma. Wake up." Blotting again, she noted that his head wound didn't look bad enough to have made him lose consciousness, despite the bleeding. Head wounds normally bled more than other kinds, right?

"Let me out," he said again, this time with more force.

"Joe, it's Emma. You're safe." She stopped blotting and simply cradled his cheek in her palm. "I'm here."

His eyes popped open, but she could tell he wasn't there. The force of the rage and despair in them made her feel like crying. "Joe?"

"Mama?" he whispered.

"It's Emma," she replied, still touching him.

Pushing himself off the ground, he rose, tilting his head as if listening for something. "What's going on?"

Emma followed suit, the tissue falling from her grasp. She couldn't shake the feeling that something was terribly, terribly wrong here. Normally, Joe came out of his fugue states by now. What if the memories had taken hold and refused to let go? What if he never came back? "Joe, what did that man say to you?" she whispered.

With a cry that was pure rage and despair, Joe lunged for her, pinning her with his body and smacking the palms of his hands hard on the wall surface on either side of her head. She winced at the sound of the impact.

"Let me out!"

"Joe," she said, though barely any sound emerged from her throat.

His golden eyes focused then, looked right at her, but the emotion, the pure hatred in them frightened her to her core. He still wasn't there.

"I'll kill you," he said in a low growl. "I swear, if you've hurt her, I'll kill you with my bare hands."

"Joe," she repeated, her voice stronger now. Her can of pepper spray lay on the ground, well out of her reach, but if she had to, she knew of at least twenty places she could punch, kick or jab to incapacitate and get free of him. God, she hoped it didn't come to that.

Then his face crumpled, his shoulders

sagging. "Somebody, let me out," he said brokenly.

Her fear left as suddenly as it had come. After all, he was still Joe, even if he was in some altered state. Reaching up, she cupped his beautiful face with her hands and did the only thing she could think of to bring him back. She kissed him, a light press of her lips to his.

He kissed her back.

"I'm here," she whispered against his mouth. "It's Emma."

She felt him blink, his lashes brushing against her cheek. He tried to pull back, but she gripped the back of his neck and kissed him again. "Joe, I'm here."

His hands fell from where he'd planted them beside her head, with a force that could have smashed her skull, and he skimmed her arms with a gentleness that nearly undid her. Down to her wrists, then back up again, to her bare shoulders, up her neck, into her hair. "Emma. Oh, Emma," he murmured, kissing her again. "Don't remember, don't ever remember," she heard him whisper.

They remained like that, kissing for

awhile, until Emma pulled away. "Joe, what happened? What—?"

He skimmed his hand along her chin, his eyebrows drawing together. "You're shaking," he said, a question in his eyes.

"I'm fine. How—?"

"I'm sorry." He dropped his hand and backed away, so she was leaning on one wall and he was standing against the opposite one.

Emma squinted at him in puzzlement. He wouldn't have known what he had done, would he? "For what?"

"I scared you. And rightfully so." He shoved his hands into his pants pockets, worry lines on his forehead showcasing his regret.

That wasn't right. Normally, Joe had no recollection of what he did when his mind went underground. "You remember?"

He nodded. "I remember. Everything."

THEY WALKED BACK to the car in silence, Emma chewing on her lip again but refraining from asking him just what the "everything" was that he'd recalled.

He wanted to tell her, but the words refused to come. It was as if his mind would only communicate in pictures now, play-by-play visions of the night his mother had been murdered. It had all come back in a rush while he'd grappled with the Whistling Man, so suddenly and vividly that he'd completely lost control.

How long would this go on? How many times would the brutal avalanche of memories keep assaulting him, pushing him down into a place where he was simply an observer, watching his body act while his mind broke down? His brothers, his baby sister, his father…he remembered all of it. And those memories corroborated the Whistling Man's assertion that he'd murdered Joe's parents. He remembered that voice.

But what they didn't tell him was under whose orders the man had acted.

So he wasn't much closer to uncovering the mystery behind his parents' death than he had been a few days ago. But what he did know was that he was becoming dangerous. He could have seriously hurt Emma, all because when the memories came, he had only a vague sense of the world around him, and in that state, everything seemed threatening. Including her.

You're weak. You should have let her go a long time ago, and you didn't. And now she was in danger from both sides—his parents' killer and from Joe himself.

Swallowing a curse, Joe reached out and took the car keys from Emma's hand, careful not to touch her skin, and unlocked the driver's side door for her.

"Thank you," she said softly, searching his face as if trying to read his mind.

Taking care to keep his expression blank, Joe dropped the keys back into her outstretched hand. Chewing on her bottom lip, as he now knew she often did when confused or upset, she tossed her small handbag into the passenger seat.

Hope you like your present.

The man's words came back to Joe in stark clarity, and he knew better than to dismiss the rumblings of his intuition. Something was wrong here. What was he missing?

More important, what had the man been doing in the garage, near their car?

Emma gripped the top of the car door.

He'd left a note, but was that all?

She put one foot inside.

Why had he been waiting by the stair-well?

Using the door for balance, she started to fold her body into the seat.

What had he wanted to see?

Joe quickly scanned the inside the car as Emma got in, and what he saw there hit him like a slap in the face.

"Emma, no!"

Chapter Twelve

The bodyguard wiped his eyes with the back of one hand, feeling no more sensation than if Emma Jensen Reese had thrown water in his face. He crossed Grand Avenue and stepped into the shadow of an office building across from the Biltmore.

They might have thought they'd bested him, but they were wrong. He'd spent a long time developing an immunity to pepper spray, learning to fight effectively, learning to kill when his employers told him to kill.

And tonight, his employer had finally given the word.

Just as he'd predicted.

Pretty, pretty Emma. His only regret was that he wouldn't be able to spend any time with the lovely Dr. Jensen Reese. But he'd just have to console himself with watching her and her beloved Joe die.

He'd always loved to watch his own handiwork.

JOE'S ARM SHOT OUT like a striking cobra, gripping Emma under her arm with a pressure that hurt, but she could tell by the tone of his voice that he had a good reason.

"Don't sit down!"

Caught off balance and half-in, half-out of the car, she flailed her arms, catching the steering wheel with her right hand and using it to keep herself hovering above the seat. The foot inside the car buckled at the ankle, but with Joe's help, she managed to remain upright.

"What's wrong?" She felt Joe's free arm snake across her back, until it gripped her right shoulder, supporting her.

"Emma, be very, very careful. I'm going to get you out of the car now."

She felt a twinge of panic, fluttering in her rib cage like a trapped butterfly. "What is it?"

"There's a bomb in the car. It's set to go off when you sit down."

Gasping, Emma tightened her grip on the steering wheel and reached down with her free hand to grasp Joe's sleeve. She arched her back, inhaling deeply, anything to keep her as far away from the seat as possible.

"I've got you," he said, his voice deep and calm and reassuring, and she felt him take some of her weight on his arm. "I won't let anything happen to you. Just follow my directions, okay?"

At her nod, Joe continued, "I want you to slide the hand on the steering wheel towards me. Carefully."

She did what he'd asked, moving her hand down the bumpy wheel inch by agonizing inch. Fear and a deep, deep anger that someone would try to do this to her, to them, caused her breath to come out in audible gasps.

"Okay, Emma, here's the hard part. I need you to move that foot that's inside the car back out. But you can't touch any part of the seat."

"Dammit, Joe!" Frustration made her

words sharper than she'd intended. "If I hit that seat, both of us are going to die!"

"I won't let that happen." He sounded sure and strong, and even caught up in the quicksand of her fear, Emma could almost believe him.

"I'm going to do this slowly, all right? Just tell me how I'm doing," she said.

"You got it."

Moving her shoe as far toward the front of the car as she could, she slid her foot sideways an inch, her heel skidding along the rough texture of the Prius's interior carpet.

"Okay?" she asked.

"You're doing great," he said. "Relax. I've got you. Let yourself rest on my hands."

She swallowed, her heart beating in triple time. "Uh, Joe, I think you're grossly underestimating my weight."

"Relax, Emma."

She did as he asked, sliding her foot another inch closer to the door. Stopping to take a breath, she tightened her grip on the steering wheel, then moved a bit more. She felt the barest hint of a brush against her calf, and she jerked her leg toward the front of the car, knowing that she'd come perilously close to the seat.

"You're fine. Doing great, Em," he murmured.

One more inch, then another, and finally, she felt her heel connect with the metal door frame. She lifted her foot and pulled it free, stumbling backward still in Joe's arms. Neither one of them noticed as her heel caught one of the wires sticking out from under the seat until they heard the sound of the blasting cap connecting with the fuse.

JOE HAD ONLY ENOUGH TIME to pull Emma free of the car and curve his body over hers in a futile attempt to shield her from the explosion. And then...

Actually, he shouldn't have had even that much time. He'd closed his eyes as soon as he'd heard the devastating click that should have been immediately followed by fire and brimstone and bits and pieces of Emma's Prius. But unless they'd died a lot faster than he'd expected, the bomb hadn't gone off.

He opened his eyes. Emma was sitting on the garage floor underneath him, her legs splayed out in painful-looking directions. She was clinging tightly to his sleeves, her face buried against his chest.

"Emma?" he said softly. She slowly raised her head.

"We're not dead," she breathed.

"No," he said, unable to keep the wonder out of his voice.

"That son of a—ugh!" With that, Emma smacked her palms against the oily concrete and pushed herself up to a standing position. "He put a bomb in my Prius! He tried to kill us, and he put a bomb in my Prius!" With that, she stalked over to the nearest wall, planting her hands on top of it and leaning over the open-air top half. "We're still alive, you psycho," she yelled. "And I'm going to bury you, do you hear me? You'd better be prepared, because next time, I'll have more than a can of pepper spray with which to kick your sorry ass!"

And then, just as suddenly as it had come, her bravado disappeared in a slow leak, seeping the color from her cheeks and curling her body into a defeated slouch. "Oh, God, Joe, we nearly died," she said softly. Her eyes remained defiantly dry, but her hands started trembling, and then the tremor rose up her arms, until her entire body was shaking so hard, it made her teeth chatter.

Reaching for her, he pulled her into his arms, keeping her tightly against his chest as she wrapped her arms around his neck and held on. And then he had to clamp his jaw shut and tense his own muscles to keep himself from shaking, as his mind replayed the moment where Emma had almost set off the bomb again and again and again.

SEVERAL HOURS LATER, after numerous interviews with Detective Landau and various members of the LAPD, Joe helped Emma out of a taxi in front of the Century Plaza Hotel in Century City, her car having been impounded for evidence collection after a thorough going-over by the bomb squad. Detective Rodriguez had been notably absent from the entire process, and Landau told them he'd most likely want to interview them himself tomorrow. They'd told Landau everything about the evening's events, withholding only their theories about Senator Allen's involvement. Until they got to the bottom of Rodriguez's suspicious behavior, they felt it best to keep the tenuous connection they'd established between Senator Allen and the Lopezes to themselves.

Joe hadn't said much to her on the ride over, other than to initiate a brief conversation about why staying in a different location other than her house or his hotel might be a good idea. She'd tried to talk to him—about the night's events, about their future plans, even about what was going to happen to his stuff at the Holiday Inn while they hid out at the Century Plaza—but he'd managed to shut down all attempts at conversation, preferring instead to scowl out the window.

After checking into the main horseshoe-shaped building, they went up to their room, a four-star suite with a sitting room, bedroom and kitchenette. Emma immediately kicked off her black strappy sandals, reveling in the feel of the plush beige carpet underneath her sore feet.

Joe immediately moved toward the maroon couch in the sitting room. "You can have the bed," he said, breaking the silence that hung heavy between them. He flicked on one of the standing lamps next to the couch, so Emma brushed her palm against the wall switch to turn off the too-bright overhead lights.

"Okay." She watched him shrug out of his tuxedo jacket and loosen his tie, then unfasten the buttons near his collar, revealing a patch of golden skin at his throat. Then he turned away from her to toss some of the pillows that lined the back of the couch to the floor to enlarge his sleeping area.

"I think I saw some robes in the bathroom if you'd rather not sleep in your dress," he said, his back still to her. Though he'd probably intended his words to be dismissive, something in his voice drew her closer to him. Reaching out, she ran her palms up his back, and she felt him shudder slightly at her touch.

"Tell me what you remember," she said, not a doubt in her mind that the memories that had come back to him tonight were what took up his thoughts now.

He moved forward, past the couch to the large window on the other side of the room. She joined him, staring out at the Shubert Theater across the street, where a revival of the musical *Chicago* was playing. The ABC Entertainment Center sat next to the Shubert, and just a few blocks down, a black-and-white sign marked the entrance to Fox Studios.

After a few minutes of silence, during which Emma could practically feel the tension coming off him, Joe spoke, so softly she had to lean forward to hear.

"I remember my father was shot by a sniper three days before my mother died. It happened while he and his partner were making an arrest—two men were robbing a gas station. The police decided the gunman must have been acting as a lookout, though they never caught him. The two they arrested denied there was ever a third gunman." He rested his forearm against the windowpane and leaned his forehead against it, still staring outside.

"My parents fought a lot before he died," he continued. "My mother kept sending us to Jasmine Bernard's. She'd tell me to watch over my brothers and sister, and she'd stay in the house by herself. The night she was killed, I went over there because I missed her, and I didn't understand what she was doing. You know the rest— she hid me behind that secret panel in the living room and wasn't able to protect herself when her killer showed up." He scrubbed a hand across his face. "I remember shouting myself hoarse when the panel wouldn't open, and then I fell asleep. When I woke up, Louis was there. He carried me out, and I remember seeing my mother's hand, palm up. The rest of her was hidden behind the couch. I think Louis moved her."

Moving behind him, Emma encircled his waist with her arms, pressing her cheek between his shoulder blades. He straightened, the muscles in his back tensing at her touch, but she still held on.

"The man who attacked us tonight killed her. His voice—it brought everything back, even if he hadn't told me he'd done it. It was like a goddamned movie, and I couldn't stop it, couldn't even function while it was going on. And it felt like she'd just died, at that very moment, even though it happened over twenty years ago."

He turned to face her, that too-familiar haunted look in his eyes. "I almost hurt you," he said, his jaw so tense, he'd practically ground the words out. "I'm sorry."

"You didn't. I could have gotten away from you at any time," she whispered. When he tried to pull out of her arms, she moved with him, refusing to let him go. "I could have gotten away," she repeated.

"I've always had everything under control. I thought I was fine. And this…" He scowled up at the ceiling, blew out a breath. "If I leave you, you have no protection. If I stay with you, I'm putting you in more danger." He tilted his head until his forehead was touching hers. "You need to get away from me," he whispered. "Start your fall break early. Go somewhere nice. I'll buy your tickets. Just get away."

She reached up and cupped his cheek, her forehead still touching his. "No."

"I need you safe."

"I need you." Pulling back slightly, she looked at him as she said the words. He seemed more tense than ever, but there was a flicker of something else in his expression, too—something that gave her the courage to keep going. "Everyone in your life has left you somehow," she said. "I won't do the same." The hand on his cheek brushed back his thick, glossy hair.

"Emma, don't."

"Stop me," she challenged.

"You don't want to do this." His head was turned slightly away from her, his eyes focused on a spot on the wall, as if it held all the answers to his questions. But he hadn't pulled away from her yet.

"How long have you been living your life on the surface, Joe?" she asked. "How many people have you pushed away? You think just because you have a big emotion that I'm going to run from you?" She moved into his line of vision, forcing him to look at her. "You remembered your brothers and your sister tonight, too, didn't you?"

His mouth twisted, and she knew she was right. "But you didn't even mention them," she went on, "because you're working so hard to push those memories away. And I don't blame you. You had more pain to deal with at ten than a lot of us have in a lifetime, and you dealt with it then the best you could. And I'm so sorry that that means it's all coming back full force now, that you're losing your family all over again. But you won't lose me."

She took his face in her hands. "You can't push me away, Joe. I care about you, and I am *not* leaving you."

"Emma." His voice broke as he finally met her eyes.

"I'm here, Joe," she whispered.

"I don't—"

She put her hand over his mouth, stopping his words. "I'm not leaving."

He moved her hand away, then just

looked at her for a long time. Then, without warning, his mouth came down on hers.

She'd expected a hard kiss, one with the strength of his emotion behind it, but he kissed her softly, with a gentleness that made her wonder how long she could keep standing.

"Emma," he breathed against her lips. He reached up and pulled the pins out of her hair, one by one, until her hair fell loose over her shoulders. And still he kept kissing her, gently nibbling her lips and teasing her with his tongue. He smoothed his hand across her shoulder, until the strap of her dress fell down her arm, and then repeated the action with the other strap.

Her fingers went to the buttons of his shirt.

He pushed her dress down her arms. She hadn't been able to wear a bra, since the back was cut so low, so when the material hit her waist, she heard him inhale sharply. Reaching up, he traced her collarbone with light, butterfly touches, tracing a line from the hollow of her throat in between her breasts. Then, he pulled her to him and lowered his head to kiss her neck.

"Joe," she whispered, unfastening the last of his shirt buttons. She tugged the material free of his waistband, then ran her hands up his tanned chest. Dear heaven, the man had washboard abs, and here she was, still standing in a pair of control-top nylons that were squeezing her hips as if she were a six-foot sausage. Her hands jerked away and went to her dress as if they wanted to cover her up of their own will.

His head came up and his mouth quirked up in his signature half smile, as if he knew exactly what she was trying to do. "I love that dress," he said into her ear, then caught her earlobe between his teeth. "I'd love you out of it more."

She gasped as goose bumps rose all across her skin from his kisses.

Somewhere, in the back of her mind, Emma would have liked to argue that point, but she found she couldn't. All she wanted was to enjoy this moment, to feel and breathe and taste all of Joe that she possibly could. Reaching back, she undid the small zipper that lay hidden by folds of material at the small of her back. Stepping away from him, she hooked her thumb into the waistband of her panty hose and tugged, lifting her legs until both they and her dress were lying in a pool at her feet.

Joe's whiskey-colored eyes grew heavy-lidded, and the half smile was still playing about his lips. "You're beautiful, Em," he murmured. "You take my breath away."

And then she was in his arms again, kissing him as if she'd never stop. He shucked his shirt in one easy movement, then reached down and caught her behind her knees, swinging her up into his arms as if she weighed nothing. She would have protested, but his mouth was still on hers, and she found her own breath stolen by the incredible sensation of his smooth, bare skin against hers.

Joe carried her into the bedroom, depositing her gently on the bed as if she were made of glass. He moved over her then, his thick, glossy hair falling into his eyes. She brushed it back, then tangled her hands in it and brought his face to hers. And then Joe showed Emma what the most erotic night of her life could really be.

Chapter Thirteen

Joe woke up from the best night of his life with the clear, unadulterated knowledge that it had been a huge mistake.

The first rays of sunlight filtered through the filmy curtains, and although he'd probably gotten about an hour's sleep, he felt rested, peaceful.

Like he'd come home.

He sat up in bed, the sheet falling down to his waist, and watched Emma sleep. She was on her stomach, her face turned toward him and her hair streaming back in a golden-brown cascade on the pillow. He shifted his weight slightly, and his movement caused her to stir. Eyes still closed, she patted the mattress until her hand connected with his thigh. Smiling contentedly, she snuggled deeper into the sheets, let out the mother of all snorts, and then her breathing assumed its regular sleep pattern.

Ah, Emma. Brave, fierce, loving Emma.

Leaving her was going to hurt like hell.

But that's exactly what he had to do. She'd given him something last night. She'd made him feel loved, made him feel strong. Made him *feel* for the first time in…years. She'd been right—he had been living on the surface since his family had been pulled apart. Twenty-five years of feeling nothing but Zen-like calm and shoving everything else into the deepest recesses of his mind, all until Emma Jensen Reese had come into his life.

And now it was time to give something back.

He'd nearly hurt her last night, when his mind had taken another nosedive into the Land of Raving Insanity. And all because he'd been too selfish to let her go back when doing so could have made a difference, could have kept her safe. He hadn't been able to let go, so he'd kept coming back to her like a goddamned

Mexican lemming. He'd led his enemies right to her doorstep, and then he'd turned on her as well, intentionally or not. And he knew that if he couldn't control the memories, or himself, then he shouldn't be around her.

At the very least, his actions last night had been a sign that he needed to find his past, to finish this before he could offer her a future. But something deep inside him knew that truthfully, she deserved better.

Slowly, he peeled back the sheet and got out of bed, tucking a pillow under Emma's arm when she'd started patting the mattress in search of him. After dropping a kiss on her forehead, he moved silently across the carpet, into the living room area of the suite where he'd left his clothes. He pulled on his boxers and pants and was just stuffing his arms into his shirt when she walked out of the bedroom.

"Hey, Em," he said, lowering his eyes as if concentrating on fastening the buttons, just so she couldn't see how his heart had leapt at the mere sight of her.

"Where are you going?" Her voice was even huskier in the morning.

He finished buttoning up his shirt, then turned his attention to the cuffs. "Back into the city. I have a list of Allen's former staff members back when he was mayor, so I thought I'd start talking to them."

Her hand went to the lapels of the white hotel robe she'd put on, squeezing the thick terry cloth closed against her throat. "Do you want me to come with you?"

He shook his head. "Nah. I'll be faster alone."

She tilted her head back, looking sideways at him, that look that made him feel as if she could read his mind. "Right."

Tucking his shirt into his waistband, he picked up his jacket and tie from the couch and slung them over an arm. "I left some money for a cab for you on the table." He gestured to the small table in the breakfast nook near the suite's kitchenette. "I didn't want you to be stranded."

Her mouth twisted, and she looked up at the ceiling briefly before turning her attention back to him. "And you didn't think that would be a little insulting after last night?"

Oh, God, Em. "What about last night?" He forced himself to shrug, to adopt a casual, almost bored expression.

"What about—?" She raked a hand through her hair, causing her curls to tumble about her worried face. "Come on, Joe. We're both adults here. If you have something to say, say it.

You can do this, Lopez. Come on. Realizing he'd been about to bolt through the door without his shoes, he put down his jacket and tie and sat down to pull on his socks. "Em, last night was nice. Really. You're a great person."

She covered her eyes with her hands. "Oh, God."

Reaching for his shiny black shoes, he slipped his feet into them, then tied the laces. "I'm sorry. I just don't do relationships. Never could." His chin still lowered, he looked up at her. "It's not you. It's me." *Oh, man, her face.* He knew he'd never forget that expression, never forget what he'd done to put it there.

She turned away from him toward the window so he could only see her profile. "Of course."

It took everything he had to keep from reaching for her. "You can call my last ex, Lucy Harrington. I believe the phrase she used was 'emotionally unavailable.'" With that, he rose, tucking his tie into his pocket and slinging his jacket over one shoulder.

She turned back to face him, her green eyes on fire. He'd never been sorrier in his life.

"You mean," she said slowly, "that last night meant nothing? That you didn't feel a thing?" When he didn't reply, she went on. "I need to hear you say it, Joe."

Last night was the best night of my life, and I've wanted you since you tried to pepper spray me in your front yard.

He turned and walked to the door, every step more painful than anything he'd ever done in his adult life. His hand on the knob, he turned his head but didn't quite look at her. "Last night was nice, Emma, but it didn't mean a whole lot."

THAT WEEKEND was basically character-
ized by the highest number of mood
swings Emma had ever had in such a short
period of time. When Joe had left their hotel room, she'd felt sick with embarrassment and hurt. Then logic had taken over
on the taxi ride home, and she chewed on
the thought that his casual use-'em-and-
lose-'em attitude might have all been an
act, designed to get her out of harm's way.
Or he might have been trying to protect
himself from the possibility that someone
he cared about might leave him yet again.

But then between teaching her classes
on Monday, her logical self had taken that
train of thought one step further, forcing
her to confront the awful, awful thought
that she was just fishing for comfort and
Joe's attitude was what it was.

And interspersed throughout the whole
depressing cycle were bouts of worry over
Joe's safety. Add to that her curiosity over
whether he was making any progress interviewing Senator Allen's old staff members, and you had a bona fide mess.

But basically, the hurt and embarrassment were constants. Especially whenever one of the LAPD extra patrols he'd obviously requested drove by her house. And sometimes, she could've sworn, Joe himself.

When she arrived home on Monday evening, she grabbed a jar of chocolate-hazelnut spread out of her cupboard, got a spoon, and started to eat it plain—her standard cure for the blues. Unfortunately, even Nutella was no match for Joe Lopez.

When she was about a quarter of the way into the jar, the doorbell rang, causing her pulse to quicken into a machine-gun pace. Joe.

Leaving the jar with the spoon stuck in it on top of her counter, she licked her lips and made her way to the door. Just as she reached it, she paused, making her way back to the small table in the corner of her sitting room to pick up her cordless phone handset. If it wasn't Joe at the door, it might be someone she'd need to escape from in a hurry, thank you very much, Mr. Lopez.

Carefully peering through an opening in the side window curtain, she jerked her body back behind the door when she saw who it was, flattening it against the heavy wood.

Detective Rodriguez. And he was alone.

"Dr. Jensen Reese?" she heard him call. He rapped his knuckles against the small, diamond-shaped glass window in the top center of the door.

She didn't respond. Maybe if she ignored him, he'd go away. A cop wouldn't break in in broad daylight, would he? Not even a corrupt cop would be so bold.

He rapped once more. Then again…

"Dr. Jensen Reese, I can see your hair through the glass," he called.

Instinctively, Emma ducked, pressing her hand on top of her head. But she knew it was too late. Undoing the locks, Emma pulled open the door and quickly stepped outside onto her front stoop. If Rodriguez wanted to do anything, he'd have to do it in front of her neighbors.

He was wearing a dark gray suit today, with a blue shirt and monochromatic tie. The mirrored aviator sunglasses were firmly in place, sunlight glinting off their mirrored surfaces.

Rodriguez cleared his throat. "Dr. Jensen Reese, I'm officially here to talk with you about what happened last night at the Biltmore's parking garage, but first, unofficially, I think I owe you an apology."

Now that was a surprise. "For what?" She folded her arms, leaning against the doorjamb and giving Rodriguez her scary professor face. This was definitely getting interesting.

"I've been acting—" he blew out a breath and raked his hand through his close-cropped, black hair "—less than professional, and... Well, I know you saw me following your car last night, and I just wanted to explain. I'm not who you probably think I am."

With that, he reached up and squeezed the bow of his sunglasses with his thumb and forefinger, pulling them off his face.

When he looked up at her again, Emma felt a chill work its way up her spine, sending goose bumps down her arms and across her body. "Oh, my God."

She had to call Joe.

Chapter Fourteen

"Joe, I swear to God, if you don't get your sorry self to my house right this minute, I will hunt you down and finish what I started when I tried to pepper-spray you."

He had to give it to Emma, she wielded verbal threats like a Mafia don, and though he'd vowed just this morning to stay away from her, Joe found himself pulling his rental car up in front of her house. Most of the people on his list had been dead ends anyway, except for Sheila Jones, Allen's old secretary. He couldn't help but feel that she knew more than she was saying, but it was clear that she didn't trust him as far as she could throw him. And he'd been in no mood to try to charm any information out of her.

He knocked on her door. He'd expected

her to do or say a lot of things, but grabbing him by the lapels and literally dragging him inside had not been not one of them.

"Emma, jeez," he said. "What's going—?" His words died as Detective Rodriguez stepped into his line of vision. "What…?"

The man's omnipresent sunglasses were hooked into the front pocket of his shirt, and the mere act of looking into his eyes hit Joe like a punch to the solar plexus. It was like looking at a mirror—they were the same shade of golden-brown as his own. And then, without his mind fogging over, without an avalanche of memories threatening to bury him, Joe felt a single lightning burst of recognition.

"Danny," he choked, unable to say anything else.

"Where have you been?" Daniel asked.

Joe shook his head, feeling painful pinpricks of sensation behind his eyes. "Long story," he said. "I'm sorry."

If he'd been thinking, he wouldn't have tried to embrace Daniel, not without launching into a drawn-out apology for finding every missing person under the sun but his brothers. But he wasn't thinking, couldn't think. So he just moved forward and held his brother tightly for the first time in twenty-five years.

"Where have you been, brother?" Daniel said, holding onto Joe just as tightly as Joe was holding onto him. "Where have you been?"

They remained like that for a long time, and Joe heard Emma slip out of the room. As soon as he could speak again, he stepped back. "You don't know how good it is to see you."

"Patricio lives here, too. He's not going to believe you." Daniel gave him a shaky grin.

"Crap." Joe swiped at his face with the back of his hand, wiping the dampness away. "You wouldn't think it to look at me now, but I'm known for my Zen-like calm."

Daniel's own eyes were unnaturally bright. "Yeah, me, too."

They laughed, and then Joe asked about Patricio. "He's here? Can we call him?"

Daniel gritted his teeth and inhaled through them, the sound filled with regret. "He's in Seattle. Patricio runs a personal security agency, mainly for Hollywood types. Some movie star is always making him run all over the country." Seeing the disappointment Joe couldn't hide, Daniel added, "I'll call him. I'll get him home, José."

Joe was just about to tell him he'd anglicized his name, but then he realized he didn't mind. "So you two, you were together?"

Daniel nodded. "Yeah, we were adopted by the same family."

Hope swelled in Joe's chest. "And Sabrina?"

His brother shook his head. "We know she was adopted by an out-of-state family, but that's all we know."

Joe digested that bit of information, then finally asked the question that had been uppermost in his mind since he'd first seen Daniel that day. "How long have you known who I was?"

Daniel's mouth tightened, and he looked away for a moment. "Since I saw your picture in the paper. I just…knew. You were my big brother, the one who could run the fastest, throw the farthest. You taught me to throw a spiral pass. You could do anything. And after Mom and Dad died, you just—" Daniel pinched the bridge of his nose and inhaled sharply "—disappeared. I always expected you to come back, to come find us. We tried to find you. They told us your records had been destroyed in a fire. Sabrina's, too."

"God, Danny, I'm sorry." He couldn't believe how much of that twenty-five-year-old hurt was still apparent on his brother's face.

"And then, two weeks ago, I see this picture in the *Times* with your name under it, and I thought maybe, at last, you were coming back." He laughed bitterly. "So I started skulking around the house like some crazed perv, waiting for you. And when I finally saw you, you didn't recognize me. God, that sounds stupid, now that I've said it."

"Danny, I have to tell you—"

"I know," Daniel interrupted. "Dr. Jensen Reese told me about the amnesia. Who'd've thought the Lopez brothers could have starred in their very own *telenovela*?" This time, Daniel's laugh was a little more genuine.

"I knew you," Joe said. "When I saw

you, somewhere in the back of my head, I knew you. It just took my conscious mind a while to catch up." He looked his brother straight in his golden-brown eyes, so like his own. "I've missed you all my life."

Daniel closed his eyes and pinched the bridge of his nose. "Dude, we have to change the subject. I've had just about all the warm fuzzies I can stand at the moment."

"No problem. But before that, I want you to know, my memory's coming back, and I remember the spiral pass now. Do you still suck?"

"Hey, I played for USC," Danny said. "Starting wide receiver. Wasn't good enough for the pros, but I had the scouts looking."

Joe snorted. "At what? How cute you looked in those tight pants? Because you threw like you were afraid of breaking a nail."

"Dude, I was five. That ball was bigger than my head."

Suddenly not in the mood to joke around anymore, Joe made a big show of studying his hands. "Wish I could have seen you play," he said softly.

Daniel was silent for a moment, but then he sat forward on the couch as if an idea had suddenly come to him. "I have video-tapes. Ten fun-filled hours of all my great-est moments, in one complete set, courtesy of my dad. Uh, my adopted dad." He re-minded Joe a little of Emma when she'd come into Joe's hotel room with tickets for the ball. "I have an apartment in La Brea. You should come over. We can grill out on the balcony."

"Any time," Joe said, and he knew he'd be watching every single moment of Dan-ny's videos before he left L.A. He looked around for Emma then, wishing she were with him, so she could get to know his brother. But then he remembered why that wasn't such a good idea.

"So," Daniel said, "Dr. Jensen Reese said you found something out about Mom and Dad?"

That morning, Joe's assistant had sent him printouts of the files from the flop-py—which was, indeed, an old-school Apple computer disk—he'd found inside the secret room of Emma's house, and Arkansas had express-mailed the photos developed from the canisters of film. He went out to his car and brought back the FedEx envelopes that contained each, handing them to Daniel and explaining where they'd been discovered.

"I suspect our parents were blackmailing Senator Allen," Joe said. Daniel reared up in surprise, his hand still stuffed inside one of the cardboard envelopes. "The floppy disk has a series of records detailing dates, times, and locations, though there's no indication of what. But the pictures tell the rest of the story."

Pulling the photos out of their envelope, Daniel flipped slowly through them, pausing to scrutinize each. Joe had already seen them—they were photos of then Mayor Allen in compromising situations with a blond woman who was not Amelia Rosemont Allen. "There are as many entries in the log as there are photos. I think each of them matches to a time, date, and place from the floppy."

Daniel whistled, long and low. "So Senator Allen was having an affair, and somehow Mom and Dad found out and started blackmailing him?"

Joe handed Daniel the "Dear Wade" letters that had been with the disk and the film. "Yeah, which gives the senator a pretty strong motive to have them killed. And he was powerful enough to have it done quickly and quietly." Joe filled him in on the events in the parking garage the night before, and his near certainty that the Whistling Man had carried out the murders, but on Allen's orders.

Daniel swore. "You know, I've been over the police records again and again. The investigators were good, but they didn't have any solid leads. This stuff would have helped. So much."

"It'll help now," Joe said. At that moment, his cell phone rang. He fished it out of his pocket and flipped it open. "Lopez."

"Joe, it's Franz." Detective Franzetti's voice was so loud, Joe had to hold the phone away from his ear.

"What took you so long?" Joe said, relieved to hear his friend's voice.

"Short-term memory moment. Working seven cases simultaneously will do that to you," Franzetti said. "So I found a pair of twins matching the information you gave me. Patricio and Daniel, born November 2, 1973. Last name—"

"Rodriguez. I know," Joe said, looking up at his brother. "He found me."

EMMA WALKED BACK into the room as Daniel and Joe were ending their conversation. The two men agreed that Joe would finish interviewing the senator's ex-employees, while Daniel would check on any progress Homicide Special had made on tracking down the Whistling Man.

Joe walked Daniel outside, and though her stomach felt as if she'd swallowed a big rock, Emma followed.

As Daniel drove off, an awkward silence descended on them.

"Well, then," Joe said, heading toward his car. "I'll see you."

"I'm going with you," Emma said softly. She followed him across the street to his car.

"Em, I don't think that's a good idea." He toyed with his key chain, not looking at her.

She headed around the car to the passenger side and waited for Joe to unlock the doors. "I don't care."

"Well, I do." He folded his arms on the car's green roof. "I need to do this alone."

God, this hurt. More than anything, she would have liked to have taken her pride and hidden in her house until Joe left the city. But she knew that wasn't what was best for her at the moment.

"And I need to go with you," she said. "You think I'm doing this so I can cling to you out of some weird female emotion over what happened Friday night?"

Joe blinked in surprise, perhaps because that was exactly what he'd been thinking.

"I'm going with you because my life is in danger, because whatever you brought to my doorstep now wants me dead, and my best chance of finishing this is to finish it with you." She moved so she stood next to the front fender, not the door, all the better to face Joe and drive her point home. "Your instincts have kept us safe this far, and I don't want to be without them right now. And what if you decide to black out again? Who's going to watch out for you with Daniel on the other side of town?"

"But—" Joe began.

"No buts." Channeling the take-no-prisoners professor she relied on when dealing with the bright and challenging young adults in her classes, she pushed on. "I need to finish this just as much as you do. And if you think your frat boy reaction to our sleeping together is going to keep me from doing that, think again."

Planting her palms on the hood of the car, Emma leaned in toward him, letting him know just how much she meant this. "And just for the record, you're not a frat boy, Joe. I know you better than that. So if you want to keep pretending that sleeping with me meant nothing, that we mean nothing, you go ahead. I'm a big girl, and I'll get over it. But I refuse to believe that my judgment is so awful. And I will not think so low of you. Now." She straightened and stepped back behind the passenger side of the car, her eyes not leaving his. "Open this door."

He swallowed, then hit the button to his automatic door locks. She got in.

They rode down June Street in silence, and Emma looked out the window instead of at him the entire time. She'd said her piece, and she'd always feel proud of herself for that. But it didn't mean that she wouldn't feel an emptiness for the rest of her life where Joe Lopez had been.

After a long ride down Wilshire and a quick turn onto the Avenue of the Stars, Joe pulled the car up in front of the Century City offices of Rumpole, Jenkins and Weiss, an entertainment law firm housed in a white stucco building with terra-cotta Spanish tiles.

"Sheila Jones used to be Allen's office manager when he was mayor," Joe said as they walked up the path to the rounded wooden door. "I talked to her this morning and got the feeling that she knew something, but she clammed up as soon as I started hinting about Allen having an affair."

Emma nodded, still not looking at him, and they entered the building, a tiny bell tinkling as soon as they'd pushed through the door.

"Hello, how may I help you?" the plump woman behind the front desk asked pleasantly. The waiting room was empty, and Rumpole, Jenkins and Weiss appeared to be busily working behind their closed office doors. For now, they had complete privacy.

"Ms. Jones—"

Her cherubic smile faded quickly into a frown as she recognized Joe from his earlier visit. "You." She tugged on the bottom of her knit Halloween-themed sweater vest, which she wore over a white T-shirt. "I told you, the mayor was very good to me, and I have nothing to say to you."

While Joe was striking out with Sheila Jones, Emma scanned the piles of paperwork on the woman's desk. On the top, a *People* magazine was opened to a "Where Are They Now?" article on various reality television personalities who had run through their fifteen minutes of fame some time ago.

"Ms. Jones, I'm sorry to bother you, but this information is very important to my current investigation," Joe said with only the barest hint of impatience.

"What are you, LAPD?" Sheila snapped.

"No," Joe replied. "I'm a private investigator from San Francisco."

She pressed her lips into a thin, stubborn line. "Let me see your P.I. license."

Joe sighed. "I showed you my license when I visited this morning."

"So? Let me see it again."

Emma leaned forward, her palms making a light smacking noise as she rested them on the top of the woman's mahogany desk. "Actually, Ms. Jones, he doesn't have one."

"What?" Joe burst out. "I do—"

Emma leaned closer to Sheila. "Can you keep a secret?"

Sheila flicked her eyes right and left, as if checking that her bosses weren't lurking in the room before she nodded. "Maybe."

"I'm Emma Jensen Reese. I work for a new cable television channel, and this is my associate, Bradley Barfenblatt." She gestured toward Joe, who winced at the name but fortunately kept quiet. "We're working on a show…" She paused, biting her lip. "Well, if I told you, it could leak to the other networks."

Sheila, apparently, was eating up Emma's story. "Oh, no, Ms. Jensen Reese, I'll keep it quiet."

"Well, basically, our cameras are following important politicians out on the campaign trail, in the office, in Washington. We want to show people how real decisions get made in D.C., and we're only showcasing the best and brightest." Emma was really warming to her topic now.

Sheila nodded enthusiastically. "Okay. So you're following Senator Allen?"

Emma beamed at her. "Exactly. He's done so much for California. That solar plan of his is truly visionary. In fact, I think—" She jumped as Joe tapped her ankle with his foot, then cleared her throat. "Yes, well, he's perfect for us. But someone has been sending us anonymous letters about Senator Allen having an affair with someone while he was mayor of Los Angeles."

Sheila gasped, pressing a hand to the grinning jack-o'-lanterns on her chest. "Surely you're not going to put that in your show?"

Emma gave her a sympathetic frown. "Unfortunately, the letters went to my bosses, not to me. They're already filming a segment on the letter writer. It's out of my hands." She shrugged, palms up toward the ceiling. "But I'm such a big supporter of Senator Allen's, I wanted to give him a chance to tell his side. Which is where you come in."

"How can I help?"

Emma leaned toward Sheila once more, lowering her voice. "Sheila, we need statements from people on the senator's side. We need to show there's more to the man than a mistake he made a quarter of a century ago."

Sheila narrowed her eyes. "Where's your camera? And what kind of name is Barfenblatt?"

"This is just preliminary research, Ms. Jones," Joe said. "We'll bring the cameras back later if we feel it's warranted." He cleared his throat. "And Barfenblatt is German."

"Huh." Sheila crossed her plump arms. "You don't look German. You look Mexican."

"He's half," Emma said quickly. "Now, Ms. Jones. Do you know anything about this alleged affair? Can we count on you?"

"You mean if I tell you what I know, I get to be on TV?"

Emma nodded, stifling the urge to raise her arms to heaven and sing hallelujah. "I'll do my best."

Sheila wrung her hands, obviously conflicted. "I'd do anything to support Senator Allen. He was very good to me when I worked for him. He did have an affair. I mean, when you're an office manager, it's impossible not to notice these things." She reached up to toy with a lock of her dyed copper hair, which was sprayed into a puffy bun. "Oh, that Mavis Richards. It'd be just like her to write those letters and try to cash in on his TV success. She trapped him, you know. He never would have gotten together with her if she hadn't been the aggressor."

Somehow, Emma highly doubted that Mavis Richards would have kept quiet for this long just to open her mouth to reality TV cameras. But Sheila, in her obvious hero worship, refused to believe that the senator had *chosen* to unzip his own pants and cheat on his wife.

"Can you identify the woman in this photo?" Joe asked suddenly, taking one of the photos he'd recently received of Allen and his paramour out of his jacket pocket.

"That's her." Sheila nodded. "She hasn't changed much. Married a plastic surgeon. Works for the D.A.'s office now."

Having gotten what she needed, Emma asked a few wrap-up questions and got them out of the legal offices without raising Sheila's suspicions.

"We'll be back with a camera," Joe said as they were leaving.

"Ah, when?" Sheila called as they started for the exit. "Can I have your card?"

Emma started to turn around, but Joe gently pushed her through the door. "Don't call us. We'll call you," he said, emphasizing the last word.

As Emma threw herself into the passenger seat of Joe's rental, she knew they couldn't get away fast enough.

"I can't believe we just did that," she said as Joe started the car and pulled away from the curb in front of Rumpole, Jenkins and Weiss's offices.

"Em, that was brilliant," he said, his eyes on the road as he drove past the office buildings and condos of Century City toward the Ten, otherwise known as the Santa Monica Freeway.

She couldn't help it. She had to preen a little. "It was, wasn't it?"

"You know it." Carefully negotiating into the right lane, Joe set the little car on the on ramp for the freeway and headed back to L.A. "Look, Em, there's something—"

"Look out!" A black SUV behind them had caught her eye in the side mirror, bearing down on them until...

Bam! Their bodies lurched forward as the sedan rammed into their rear bumper, and Emma felt her neck snap back. Just when they'd recovered from the shock, the SUV hit them again, causing

Joe to lose control of the car. They'd reached the end of the ramp, and the Focus fishtailed onto the freeway, tires squealing.

"Dammit!" Joe fought to regain control as the smell of burnt rubber permeated the car. He steered into the skid, managing to wobble the car back into a straight line. Several drivers around them honked their horns and sped up, obviously hoping to get away from them and their erratic driving. Emma craned her sore neck to get a better look at the maniac behind them.

"Joe, look out!" she said, and Joe jerked the wheel just in time to avoid a garbage bag filled with heaven knew what that someone had lost on the freeway.

The SUV matched their movement, sticking close to their tail. Suddenly, it swung out of the lane behind them and started creeping beside them.

"He's coming up on your side!" Emma shouted.

Both hands clutching the wheel with white knuckles, Joe floored the gas. The compact economy car barely began to accelerate, its small four-cylinder engine no match for the behemoth bearing down upon it.

The SUV came up beside them, and since the tinted passenger side window was rolled down, Emma could clearly see the hand aiming a gun straight for them.

"Joe!"

"I see it," Joe muttered. A fraction of a second later, he stomped on the brake. A spider web of fine fractures splintered across the surface of the Focus's windshield, stemming from a gouge in the upper right corner where the bullet had only grazed the glass, thanks to Joe's reflexes. But the combination of high speeds, gunshots and winding curves were too much for the little car, and it spiraled to the right, creating a corkscrew pattern across the two lanes.

Time slowed, and Emma saw a line of cars coming toward them, then the concrete freeway barriers. Reaching out, she smacked her arm against Joe's chest in a futile attempt to protect him from the impact. As they spun forward again, she saw the black SUV disappearing along the ribbon of highway in front of them, then a concrete barrier, then the line of cars again. Joe was shouting and giving the steering wheel small jerks as the Focus's brakes screamed. The windshield splintered some more. The barrier got closer.

And then, with a sudden jolt, the car shuddered to a stop, neatly in the shoulder of the highway, although it was facing in the wrong direction. Several cars shot past, honking their horns. One couple in a white Sebring convertible gave them the finger in tandem.

Breathing hard, Emma sank back in her seat, letting her head thump against the headrest. Joe was still leaning forward, clutching the steering wheel in a death grip.

"Em," he said quietly.

She lolled her head to the left to look at him. Her clammy skin prickled uncomfortably as the adrenaline drained away and she was left only with the knowledge that they'd had yet another near miss. "Yes?"

"Just how major of a donor are you to Allen's campaign?"

She inhaled deeply. "Well, my father set up this trust fund…"

"If Allen is in his offices, can you get me in to see him today?" he asked calmly.

"I think so. He sets aside some time every afternoon he's in the office for VIPs, including donors." She swallowed. "Joe, you can't possibly be thinking—"

"I'm going to finish this," he said, his voice flat and low. "I'll call Danny once we're in, and then the LAPD can do whatever they want, but first, I'm going to confront that bastard. This ends today."

Emma knew beyond the shadow of a doubt that that was a really bad idea. She opened her mouth to tell Joe so.

"I'm going with you," was what came out instead.

Chapter Fifteen

"You know, I don't think this is one of your better ideas," Emma said to Joe as they walked through the marble-and-chrome lobby of the building where Senator Allen had his offices. "Are you sure you don't want to give Daniel a call yet?"

Since Emma had called ahead to set up a late-afternoon appointment for them, getting through security hadn't been too difficult. After all, politicians gained voters by being accessible, especially to those who provided significant amounts of money for campaign expenses. But Emma was more than a little nervous about going to the senator's office. He probably wouldn't try to kill them in front of his staff, but she didn't think rubbing his face in the evidence they had against him was exactly prudent, either.

"I'll go call him now," Joe said. "Wait for me?" When she nodded, he ducked behind a potted palm in a corner to call his brother.

"Dr. Jensen Reese! What a lovely surprise."

Emma turned to see Amelia Allen striding toward her, wearing a ruffled white blouse and a gray pin-striped skirt. She tried not to show her surprise that Amelia had gotten her name right. "I'm so glad to see you. I talked to Wade about his hybrid incentive plans, and he said he'd be delighted to talk to you about them in person anytime, especially after all you've given us."

"Well," Emma said. "I've actually got an appointment with the senator in a few minutes to discuss a donation to that program, and—"

"Wonderful!" Amelia clapped her hands together. She gestured with her chin to where Joe stood, talking on his cell phone. "And you brought your beau with you? Such a good-looking young man, your José Javier."

"Thank you, but he's not my, uh…"

Emma hesitated over the old-fashioned word "…beau."

"I'm sure you'll take care of that soon." Amelia patted her on the shoulder, showcasing a beautiful French manicure. "Well, I must run. I want to catch a minute of Wade's time in between appointments. I'll try not to take too long." She smiled without teeth and, with a little wave, set off for the bank of elevators on the far wall.

"What was that all about?" Joe asked as he came up beside her.

"Nothing much. Just pleasantries and a thank-you for donating to 'my Wade's' campaign," Emma replied. "Ready to go?"

Joe nodded. "Let's finish this," he said.

"THE SENATOR will see you now, Dr. Jensen Reese, Mr. Lopez," the young man who was serving as one of the senator's aides said. Joe and Emma rose from the brown leather couch in the corner of the senator's waiting room and followed the young man to Senator Allen's door. The aide motioned them inside.

"Senator," he said, poking his head inside after them, "Dr. Jensen Reese and Mr. Lopez to see you."

Senator Allen put down the pen he'd been using and rose, smiling warmly. "Dr. Jensen Reese, it's always a pleasure." He shook her hand, then held his palm out to Joe. "And Mr. Lopez. Nice to see you again."

Joe fought the urge to glare at him, taking care to keep his features neutral. "Senator," he said.

Allen gestured for them to sit in two leather chairs that matched the couch outside perfectly. He pulled up a third chair, rather than sitting behind his desk, as if they were all going to have a friendly chat. He had to admit, the man's charisma was an amazing force, and he had to make himself remember that this guy had given the order for his parents' murders.

"So," Allen said, steepling his fingers under his chin and leaning back in his chair. "You wanted to know more about my solar plans. Well, I must say, I'm very excited about—"

"Actually, Senator," Joe interjected, "we're here about Mavis Richards."

Allen didn't move a muscle, his smile still fixed into place. "Excuse me?"

Emma raised her eyebrows, her forehead wrinkled with worry, but he plunged on. It was what they'd come for, after all.

"Senator," he said, "we know about your affair. We have proof."

To Joe's surprise, Allen slumped down in his seat, his hands falling onto the armrests. Looking suddenly small and old, Allen simply nodded. "So you know about Mavis," he said. "It follows that you would know. Your father was the only living soul who knew back then. I always wondered if he left something behind."

"Senator, we've given that evidence to a member of the LAPD," Emma said, sitting forward in her chair. "I want you to know that if you try anything, if anything happens to us, you're the first person he's going to look for."

Allen just nodded, his blue eyes drooping sadly. "You can do whatever you wish with that information," he said. "After Ramon Lopez died, I vowed that my days of hiding were over. It was a terrible, terrible mistake, and I paid for it a hundred times over, every time I saw how I'd hurt Amelia." He frowned, picked an imaginary piece of lint off his dark gray pants. "She never forgave me, you know. Not that I deserved it. Oh, she never said as much, but I knew."

"So my father discovered the affair and blackmailed you to keep it quiet?" Joe asked. At the senator's nod, he continued. "Was Mavis Richards in on this?"

The senator shook his head. "No," he said emphatically. "She wasn't working with Ramon, and to my knowledge, he never approached her for money. Mavis is a good person. We just both made a terrible mistake."

"How did your wife find out?"

"I told her. I was going to come clean, confess everything to the public, but Amelia said it would humiliate her." The senator's frown grew deeper, and Joe could have sworn he slumped even further down in his chair. "She asked me to pay your father off, and I did it. For her."

Allen rose and moved toward his office

window, leaning against one of the dark-paneled walls and staring out at the view of the city. "I'm getting too old to hide things anymore," he said quietly. "If you want to release the information, you're welcome to." He turned and his lips turned up in a sad smile. "Amelia would understand. And I'm close enough to retirement anyway."

This wasn't quite the reaction Joe had expected. He'd thought Allen would opt for slick denial, derisive laughter or perhaps even indignation or anger. He thought if they got lucky, Allen might stumble on his words and reveal some of the truth. Never in a million years would he have expected sad resignation.

"How did my father find out about you two?" Joe asked.

The senator tugged at his silk tie. "He saw us coming out of a hotel in San Diego and stopped to talk to us. Mavis had her guilty conscience written all over her face, and Ramon put the pieces together. He followed us, took a few pictures..."

Allen flipped a palm in the air. "You know the rest."

Joe stole a glance at Emma, who had bewilderment written all over her face. Joe turned back to Allen. "You talked about my father, Ramon. Did my mother ever...?" He paused, unable to finish the sentence.

Allen returned to the center of the room and sat back down. "No, son, your mother didn't have anything at all to do with it. I learned that later on, when I asked your father about her during one of our...exchanges. The look of panic on his face told me all I needed to know, and I told him I'd tell Daniela everything and to hell with my career if he kept up his scheme. It all ended that day."

Though part of Joe's mind was having a hard time letting go of Allen as the chief suspect in his parents' murder, every fiber of his being told him that Allen was telling the truth.

"Joe." Emma shot up from her seat. "He's telling the truth." Grabbing his arm, she pulled him toward the door, although she should have known Allen could still hear her. "When I was talking to Mrs. Allen—who has never remembered me before, by the way—she called you José Javier."

Allen's head shot up, and some of the fire came back into his blue eyes. "What are you saying, Dr. Jensen Reese?"

"I'm saying," Emma said carefully, "that I never told your wife Joe's full name. I introduced him as Joe. So she had to know somehow that this adult Joe Lopez," she gestured toward Joe, "was Ramon Lopez's son, José Javier. Or she would have called him Joe, like I did."

Allen shot up out of his chair. "I don't appreciate what you're implying. Amelia would never—"

A gunshot shattered the window just behind Joe. Just then, the Whistling Man strode into the room, brandishing a handgun.

Without thinking, Joe ran forward, tackling the man around the waist. He felt another gunshot whiz by his head as he made impact. The man buckled at his waist with an *oof* and flew against the wall, Joe still clinging to him. They both sank to the floor. Out of the corner of his eye, Joe saw the man's gun skitter across the floor; Emma immediately picked it up.

They had only lain on the floor for a moment, when the man brought his clenched hands down on Joe's back, sending sharp, brutal pain ripping through his spine. In a cloud of fury, Joe reared up and hit him square in the stomach with a jab, then pushed himself up to a standing position.

The man pushed with his arms behind his head and arched his back, flipping his legs so they supported his weight until he was standing. He circled to the right. Joe went left.

The man swung. Joe arced his body, feeling a rush of air where the man's fist nearly connected with his ribs.

And then he looked into the eyes of his parents' killer and swung. His fist connected with the man's jaw, sending him reeling backward. Joe advanced again, hitting him in the solar plexus with a one-two punch. The man staggered again, with a groan.

Swiping at a trail of blood leaking from the corner of his mouth, the man curled his arms protectively around his middle. Joe hit him with a front kick, and he slammed against the row of bookshelves behind him. Joe followed, grabbing the man by his shirtfront and slamming him against the shelves again.

"How long will you scream?" Joe growled. "Because only one of us is walking out of this office today, and it's going to be me." The man groaned, his eyes lolling, and Joe shoved him back against the unforgiving wood once more.

"Joe, don't."

Through the red haze of his fury, Joe heard Emma's soft voice. "Don't what?" he asked, his voice breaking.

She touched him then, just a hand on his arm, but it was enough to make him sane again, enough to make him feel as if he could breathe again. "Don't do what he does. Don't be a mindless killer."

He clenched the man's lapels tightly, until his short nails dug through the material and into his palms. His breathing come out in ragged gasps through his teeth.

"You're better than that."

"Damn you, Emma," he ground out.

"Let him go, Joe." She must have put down the gun she was holding, he thought, because both of her soft hands were on his shoulders, his back. "You're better than that."

With a groan, Joe pulled his hands away, then delivered one last, calculated punch to the man's chin, causing him to drop to the floor unconscious.

"Thank you," Emma said, resting her head on his shoulder.

"Yes, Joe, thank you." Amelia strode into the room and picked up the gun from the windowsill where Emma had left it. "Armand has been a loyal employee since he took care of your father for me. I'd hate to lose him to the likes of you."

Senator Allen took a step toward his wife. "Amelia, what are you doing? Who is this man? Amelia?"

"I did it for you, Wade." She pointed the gun at Joe and Emma, circling sideways until she stood only a couple of feet away from her husband. "He took care of the Lopezes, those low-class immigrants." She spat out the last word, as if it were a curse. "Blackmailing my husband, when he had such plans to do good. You could have been president, Wade, and you would have been wonderful. But those horrible people only thought about themselves, not about what was best for our country."

"Amelia, no," Senator Allen moaned softly.

"The world didn't need people like your parents. They were thieves. And you two are no better," she said, waving the gun at Joe and Emma.

"My mother wasn't involved in blackmailing your husband," Joe said calmly, his hands held up in the air, palms outward. "You killed an innocent woman."

Amelia faltered for a moment. "Why, I… Wade, she was, wasn't she? That Lopez woman? She was blackmailing you, too?"

Allen shook his head. "Amelia," he said, reaching for her, "give me the gun."

"But Wade, I was only doing what was

best. I took care of the children. I made sure they went to good families." She looked at Joe, her gun hand swinging toward Joe and Emma once more. "Beth Billings specialized in children with behavior problems. I found her for you. I made sure you went to someone who would help you. You couldn't speak."

"Amelia," Senator Allen said again. Tears running down his face, he put his hand on top of Amelia's, lowering the gun.

Amelia's perfectly made-up face crumpled. "Wade, I took care of the children. They went to good homes. I just wanted you to do everything you wanted to do." She let Senator Allen take the gun away from her. "You had such plans for lifting people up." She was sobbing now. "I wanted you to do them all."

"I know, sweetheart." Placing the gun on the table, Allen put his arms around his wife. "I know."

After removing the gun and disarming it, Joe and Emma left the room, closing the door behind them. Just then, Daniel and his partner arrived. Armed with the information Joe and Emma gave them, they arrested Amelia Rosemont Allen and her hired killer for the murders of Daniela and Ramon Lopez. With her husband at her side, Amelia confessed before she even got out of the senator's office.

Epilogue

It had been two weeks since Amelia's arrest. Though she was pleading guilty, she refused to divulge any information on the whereabouts of Joe and Daniel's sister Sabrina. Emma had given her own statement to Daniel Lopez at the offices of the Homicide Special unit and had only nodded at Joe when he passed her in the hall there to give his own. That was the last time she'd seen him.

"Emma, sweetheart," her mother said, having returned from her trip a few days before. "You're not concentrating."

Emma toyed with her wooden letters, but for the first time in her life, she couldn't think of a single word to make with them. "I know. I'm sorry, Mom."

"He's a cretin of the lowest order, and he doesn't deserve you," her mother said, putting her hand over her daughter's. "I know I told you to go have an adventure while I was gone, but really. Wasn't almost getting killed and getting involved with an emotionally unavailable jerk going a little too far?"

Emma laughed softly.

"I'm sorry about Joe, dear," Jane said. "And about Senator Allen, even. I know how excited you were about his solar plan."

Senator Allen had resigned from office immediately following his wife's arrest. He'd been the subject of quite a few of Emma's tirades lately, though Jane and Emma both knew who Emma was really angry at.

"I'm really glad you're home, Mom."

Jane Jensen Reese had been having such a good time in Taos that she'd put off going to the doctor until a few days after her very successful art show. Once she had gone, the doctor pronounced her cancer-free and in excellent health, and Jane had immediately made Ed drive her straight home, no stops other than for gas, so she could tell her daughter in person.

The news had been like a burst of sunlight after months and months of rain, and Emma had felt an indescribable joy at the news. But as elated as she'd been by the news, she couldn't help but wish that Joe were there to share it with her.

Ah, well. He wasn't ready to admit his feelings for her, if she wasn't just being delusional and he actually had any, and she was just going to have to move on.

Simple as that.

"So, I think I'm going to go hike the Inca Trail over Christmas break." She tossed a couple of letters on the board, building off of Jane's *tempest.*

"The?" Jane pushed her chair away from the table. "You've dumped your letters twice, and the best you can come up with is *the*? Forget this. I think some retail therapy is in order." She whirled around to pick up the telephone, holding the cordless hand set out to Emma. "Call Celia. We're going shopping. And Peru is a good idea, by the way."

Just then, the doorbell rang.

"That's probably her." Emma rose and went to answer it.

And she nearly fell over when she saw who was standing on her front stoop.

Wearing olive-green cargo pants and a fitted navy long-sleeve shirt, Joe smiled at her sheepishly, his hair falling into his eyes. "So, I was in the neighborhood, and…"

Emma folded her arms and glared at him.

"Who is it, Emma?" her mother called from the kitchen.

"Salesman," she called over her shoulder, still glaring at Joe. "Let me just get rid of him." She started to close the door, ignoring the fact that her heart was threatening to leap out of her chest.

"Em," he said quietly, holding out a hand to stop her. "I'm sorry. You don't know how sorry I am." When she stopped trying to crush him with the door, he shoved his hands in his pockets. "You were right. About everything. I was scared, and I thought… I thought I'd hurt you during one of those damn blackouts I kept having. I wanted to keep you safe, so I told you…" he raked a hand through his hair, blowing out a breath "…some really stupid things. But the truth, the truth that I've been living with ever since I went back to San Francisco, is that I love you."

She jerked back, stunned.

"I think I've loved you since you tried to Mace me. And if you let me, I'll spend the rest of my life making up for every stupid thing I said that morning."

"Joe." She put a shaking hand to her mouth, unable to believe what he was telling her.

He stepped into the house, put his arms around her and touched his forehead to hers. "You showed me that I didn't have to live on the surface, and now I don't want to stop. I love you." He kissed her then, softly, gently, as tears streamed down her cheeks. "Marry me." He dug into his pocket, pulling out a small velvet box. "I got you a vintage Victorian ring. Matches the house and no extra mining or resources were required to make it. And don't worry about leaving your house. I know you love this place, and I'll love living here as long as you're in it."

Emma sobbed through her laughter.

Just then, Daniel came bounding up the steps, followed closely by a carbon copy of himself with gelled, spiky hair. "Hey, bro," Daniel called. "Did she say yes? Because we're going to kick your ass if you managed to blow this one."

Swiping at her eyes and still holding onto Joe, Emma studied the two men before her. "Patricio?" she asked Daniel's double.

All three brothers nodded, and she could feel the strength of the connection between them. "So?" Patricio asked, an expectant look on his face. "Danny said you might have blown it, Joe, but..."

"She said yes," Emma replied, and then she was caught up in three pairs of arms, welcoming her to the family.

* * * * *

Don't miss the next book in
Tracy Montoya's brand-new series,
MISSION: FAMILY, *NEXT OF KIN,*
featuring Daniel Rodriguez.
Coming next month only from
Harlequin Intrigue!

eHARLEQUIN.com

The Ultimate Destination for Women's Fiction

Your favorite authors are just a click away
at www.eHarlequin.com!

- Take a sneak peek at the covers and
  read summaries of **Upcoming Books**

- Choose from over 600
  author **profiles!**

- Chat with your favorite authors
  on our **message boards.**

- Are you an author in the making?
  Get advice from published authors
  in **The Inside Scoop!**

**Learn about your favorite authors
in a fun, interactive setting—
visit www.eHarlequin.com today!**

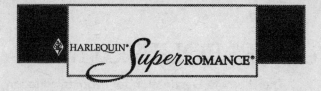
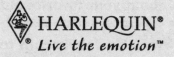

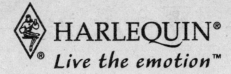
HARLEQUIN®
Live the emotion™

AMERICAN *Romance*® Upbeat,
All-American Romances

flipside Romantic Comedy

Harlequin Historicals® Historical,
Romantic Adventure

HARLEQUIN®
INTRIGUE Romantic Suspense

HARLEQUIN®
HARLEQUIN ROMANCE® The essence of
modern romance

HARLEQUIN®
Presents Seduction and passion
guaranteed

HARLEQUIN® *Super* ROMANCE® Emotional,
Exciting, Unexpected

Temptation. Sassy, Sexy, Seductive!

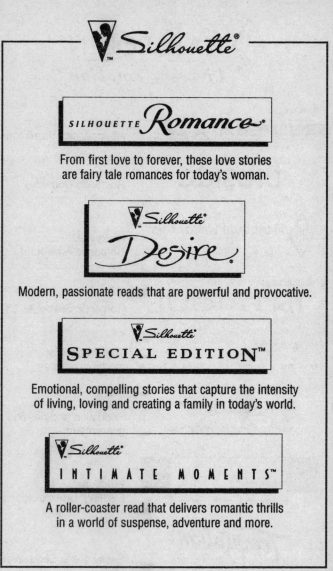

SILHOUETTE _Romance_

From first love to forever, these love stories
are fairy tale romances for today's woman.

Silhouette
Desire

Modern, passionate reads that are powerful and provocative.

Silhouette
SPECIAL EDITION™

Emotional, compelling stories that capture the intensity
of living, loving and creating a family in today's world.

Silhouette
INTIMATE MOMENTS™

A roller-coaster read that delivers romantic thrills
in a world of suspense, adventure and more.